# THE

# BELLS

*of*

# HERKIMER

NATALIE MERHEB

Published by Pewter Press

Third Edition

ISBN 978-0-9802293-7-0

Book cover by Damonza

# CHAPTER 1

Torrential rain beat relentlessly down, its rhythmic assault dancing off the plane's exterior as we swam through the sky like a giant airborne fish.

"The captain would like you to buckle up, Miss Worthington." Rebecca, the stewardess, shuffled past me to take a seat. "It doesn't look like this weather is going to le—"

Suddenly, the cabin hiccuped, sending her crashing forward, her side smashing into the leather armrest. She winced and clutched her ribs.

I reached out a hand to help her up.

"Damn turbulence," she said with a stiff laugh.

"Are we almost there?" My voice came out as a dry whisper. School let out only yesterday and instead of sleeping in after a grueling week of finals, I was on my way to my grandparents' estate in Hyannis Port to attend a fundraising gala for my father—an event he'd insisted for weeks his campaign needed. Now I wondered if I would get there in one piece.

Turbulence continued to rattle through the aircraft. I glanced out the window just as a crack of sheet lightening illuminated the cabin. A sky-shattering clap followed, and the plane plummeted.

My hands flew up, releasing the death grip I'd held on the armrests. "Rebecca!" A whooshing sound filled my ears.

"Hold on!" she cried as the cabin lights flickered.

It took only seconds for the plane to level, but I remained paralyzed in my seat, my eyes unblinking.

Rebecca was at my side immediately. "Miss Worthington! Are you all right?"

I slowly turned towards her. My head had been jerked forward so suddenly that I felt the immediate effects by way of a headache forming at the base of my skull. Rebecca looked flustered. Her hair had fallen out of the bun at the base of her neck. Her shirt was partially untucked, her face pale.

"What happened?" I managed.

"The weather caused a brief interference with the captain's controls." She paused to compose herself and in a low voice said, "I know your father has a big event but if you ask me, we should not have flown this morning."

I nodded in agreement, then sunk deeper into my seat.

Eventually, the captain's voice came over the speaker. "We are thirty miles away from the airport and will be landing shortly. Please remain seated and stay buckled."

Ten minutes later, the plane landed with a heavy bump, the tires screeching in protest as the aircraft hurriedly braked. Only when we were slowly taxiing across the tarmac did I allow myself to turn toward the window. It was overcast in Hyannis Port, Massachusetts, and gray clouds loomed low over the vast stretch of trees surrounding the small airport.

Finally, we rolled to a stop. Rebecca unlatched the door and lowered the stairs while I straightened up my area as best as I could and gathered my belongings.

I stood, my legs spaghetti, and headed for the exit, a quivering hand pulling my small suitcase behind me. I said goodbye to Rebecca and the pilots as I tried not to think about how I was scheduled to fly again tomorrow when I was to return back to New Hampshire. Clearly even the worst weather would not delay the flight if my father gave it a go.

As I descended the steps, my grandparents' driver waved at me from the rain-soaked tarmac. The gray-haired, heavy-set man who had worked at Greyhurst for as long as I could remember should have retired by now; he was well into his sixties, with an ailing wife at home and three grown children who had moved out of state. But it was no secret that my grandparents valued loyal staff, so I imagined he was paid well to stay on.

Bill smiled and held the umbrella over my head. "Nice to have you back, Miss Worthington. Let me take your bag."

"I've got it," I offered as I loaded my suitcase into the trunk of the black Mercedes. Bill closed the trunk, and I stepped over a puddle and hopped into the back seat, never so thankful to be on solid ground in my life.

On the ride to Greyhurst, we passed the large, tasteful homes of the posh coastal town, and I nervously gave myself a once over while filling Bill in on the flight from hell. To avoid my grandmother's inevitable lecture on how badly I disgraced the family name, I had traded sweatpants for a dress and made sure my nails were trimmed short and neutrally polished. My long brown hair was slicked back into a tight bun, my usual hoop earrings replaced with pearl studs.

The car crept up on an intersection surrounded by quaint brick sidewalks and the shops that lined Hyannis Port's business district. At any decent hour, Main Street would be packed with tourists and townspeople browsing in the shops and savoring the local cuisine. Now, though, perhaps because of the weather or the hour, the streets were mostly empty. That is, until we pulled up to the stoplight in front of Finnie's Finest, the town's trademark café, which doubled as an antique store.

A group of twenty or so people stood together at the street corner, holding umbrellas. As our car drew closer, I leaned towards the passenger side door, pressing my face against the window. At the sight of our car the crowd raised signs and chanted words I couldn't make out. Most of the signs showed a picture of my father, his face crisscrossed with bold red lines, the words written far from kind.

*Worthless Worthington.*
*War on Worthington, not on workers.*
*NOT MY GOVERNOR!*

I gasped and sank into the backseat. "What's going on, Bill?"

He gave them a quick glance and shook his head. "Your father is trying to bring about a lot of positive changes, but not everyone sees it that way." He adjusted the rearview mirror to make eye contact with me. "For a small town, his event tonight is big news. At the end of the day, it's politics, dear, and no one remains unscathed in politics."

Mortified as I was, I couldn't look away. Standing in the rain were men and women, young and old. Almost everyone was actively protesting in some way, either chanting or shouting or hiding behind a sign. My eyes locked with an older man who stood on the sidelines, a grey umbrella in his hands. Unlike the others, he didn't seem involved in the protest, but he made no attempt to distance himself from the group. For this group to be standing in the rain so early in the morning meant they were clearly passionate about their message—and their strong dislike of my father.

The light changed, and the car pulled away, but I knew Bill was right. This wouldn't be the last time something like this happened—the whole town was bustling about my father's candidacy. So far, the preliminary numbers indicated he had a good lead. And even if fate didn't let him become governor of Massachusetts, I knew that defeat—and my grandmother's incessant prodding—would only spur him to launch another political campaign that would leave him just as distracted and absent as he'd always been.

A short while later, we drove through the wrought iron gates of the fifty-room Worthington summer estate, set on twenty-five acres overlooking the Atlantic. Built in the late 1800s by the wealthy Massachusetts businessman Abraham Cabot, the three-story mansion was one of the most talked-about properties on the East Coast.

I was no stranger to such opulence; my family owned some of the nation's largest properties along the Eastern Seaboard. Greyhurst paled in comparison to my grandparents' main residence in Newport, and that was saying something. Buying real estate was something of a hobby—a competition even—for my absurdly wealthy relatives.

The car door opened, and Bill's white-gloved hand appeared. I reached for it, and he pulled me gently to my feet.

"Thank you, Bill," I said as I smoothed my dress.

A set of wide steps led up to the entrance, and before I reached the top step, the massive front door opened.

"Welcome, Miss Worthington," the butler said.

And, just like that, so began the most dangerous summer of my life.

ONCE INSIDE, THE housekeeper, Tillie, escorted me to my room on the second floor and began unpacking my suitcase. I wouldn't be here long enough to bother, but I left her to it and looked around.

In one corner was a floor-length navy chiffon dress that had been steamed and put on a dress form for tonight's event. On the vanity sat boxes of accessories and shoes, no doubt expertly selected to go with the dress. A small card with my name handwritten on the front lay on top of one of the boxes.

*Meredith,*
*I trust that the staff has seen to your every need. Please make yourself at home and forgive me for not being there to welcome you. Your father and I are seeing to a prior commitment and will return later this afternoon.*
*Regards,*
*Agnes*

"So much for not sleeping in," I muttered, returning the card to its place. I knew my father had

gala preparations and campaign business to attend to—
he'd flown in late last night, and I didn't plan on seeing
him until the second he was announced on stage
tonight—I just didn't know my grandmother had taken
it upon herself to accompany him.

I made my way to the bathroom to splash water on
my face. After freshening up, I pulled my hair out of
the scalp-numbing bun and into a ponytail—how not a
single hair had jumped out of place after that flight was
beyond me. Then I paused in the full-length mirror to
wonder once again if my knee-length peach cotton
dress and favorite white ballet flats were going to be
deemed too short and too casual. The last thing I
needed was to be cast in the same bracket as Priscilla
Hubbard, whose support hose showing under her inch-
too-short skirt was, according to my grandmother, an
event so scandalous it was right up there with the
invention of email. I didn't want to hear the lecture
later, so after sashaying back and forth with great force
and testing that my hem was long enough, I grabbed a
magazine I'd packed and moseyed out the door, down
the winding stairway, and through the foyer.

Despite the absence of my family, the house was
bustling with people helping set up for tonight's event.
Florists carrying large arrangements scurried toward the
ballroom, eager young men with banners and campaign
décor following closely behind. Everything looked fit
for a Worthington gala; the elaborate banister looked
deliberately more polished today, the floors glistened
and gleamed like mirrors.

But it wasn't just the floors my grandmother would
want pristine. Soon the glam crew would arrive and
start working me from the feet up, leaving no hair out
of place, no eyelash uncurled, no folds in my dress. It

9

would surely be an afternoon-long process, so despite the gloomy weather, I slipped outside, not wanting to be in anyone's way as they set up.

The clouds hung low and ominous, obscuring the sun. In the distance, the storm that we had just flown through was quickly making its way south, so I knew my time outside was numbered. Magazine in hand, I continued down the walkway that cut through the lush, manicured lawn to the path flanked with pale pink trees flowering on each side. When I finally exited the long-shaded canopy, I walked through the flower gardens, past the stargazer lilies and delphinium.

Only inches from the dock, my foot caught on an uneven patch of grass and the magazine fluttered from my grasp as I landed with my palms in the dirt.

"Classy," I muttered as I picked myself up off the ground. My pastel dress was streaked with brown smut, my white shoes hardly colorless anymore.

"Are you okay?" a distant voice asked.

I spun around to see a guy who looked to be around my age rushing toward me. He had short dark hair and was dressed in faded jeans and a T-shirt with a utility belt around his waist.

"Let me get that for you," he offered as he reached down and picked up my magazine. "Here," he said, straightening the bent pages and handing it to me. "Oh, damn. Your knee—"

I looked down to see blood dripping out of a large gash on my knee.

"Wait here, I'll be right back." Then he darted off toward the shed.

I opened my mouth to protest, but he was already gone.

Glancing down at my leg, I wondered if I should wait for this stranger to return or go back inside and treat it myself. Before I had time to give it much thought, he was back carrying bandages and wipes.

"Here, sit down and I'll get you cleaned up," he said, wiping leaves off the bench next to me and gesturing toward it.

I sat, feeling much too close to someone whose name I didn't know. He quickly got to work wiping my knee with a disinfectant.

"Sorry," he said when I winced.

"I don't believe we've met," I said through gritted teeth.

"Jack Saunders. I maintain the property for Mr. Worthington."

"I'm Meredith, his granddaughter."

"Nice to meet you." He paused awkwardly. Once the cuts were cleaned, he put a large bandage over the area and took a step back. "There. Again, I'm really sorry about that. I'll make sure we block off this area until we get that patch taken care of."

"Thank you," I murmured as I surveyed his handiwork. "How long have you worked here?" The prospect of having a new landscaper wasn't surprising; unlike Bill, newer staff didn't carry any weight with my grandmother, and the turnover rate was high.

"A little over a week now . . . summer job. I'm trying to acclimate to life in Massachusetts before I start college in the fall."

"That's nice. Where did you move from?"

He chuckled. "A really, really small town in northeast Canada."

"I see. And where are you headed come fall?" I sucked at introductions.

"Harvard."

My eyes grew wide. The gardener was going to Harvard?

"I know, I probably am better suited at the community college, huh?"

My face flushed. "No, of course not." The longer the idea simmered, the more I realized that my reaction had been hasty. Good for him if he had the chance to go to an Ivy League school.

I looked down at my dirty shoes. "My family boasts a long line of Harvard graduates, all of whom studied law. I keep telling myself I'll be the first to break the mold. I would much rather get into healthcare than politics. Let's just say I've only got a year to muster the courage."

"A lot can change in a year," he suggested, shoving his hands into his pockets.

"Very true. I guess I'll have to wait and see what happens." I stepped onto the dock and looked out at the dark waters that rose in swells and crashed against it. Grey clouds overhead rolled through the sky, and a cool breeze from the ocean whipped my hair. There, off to the east side, my gaze settled on the distant island upon which sat the Herkimer mansion.

The Herkimer mansion was a striking Victorian manor with a heartbreaking history. Commissioned by a wealthy resident sometime in the 1800s, the house had never been lived in. The story goes that it was originally intended to be a gift for the man's wife and was near completion when she suddenly died. Construction was halted, and legend has it that he never set foot on the island again. The house had been passed down to his family over the generations, but no one ever resided there. A mysterious fire many years ago that consumed the entire west wing only confirmed what the locals had said all along: the house was cursed. It had since been condemned, waiting for the family to tear it down. Nevertheless, Herkimer was the closest thing my grandparents had to visible neighbors.

"So what's the story with that house?"

When I told him, he laughed. "Cursed. Haunted. Those are just words people make up when they're hiding something."

Unsure why I sensed the need to defend the story, I replied, "Given the circumstances, I'd say it certainly seems cursed."

He frowned. "You've been there?"

"It's private property, the sign is practically visible from here," I said. What I failed to mention was that in many ways it felt as if I had been there. Dreams of Herkimer had plagued me since I was a child. In them, I am walking around the house in circles, a pilgrimage of sorts. But I never step inside. "Plus, if it is cursed or haunted or whatever, I wouldn't want to take my chances."

"And to think, you might be able to dispel the old wives' tales." He winked.

"Who are you, one of the Hardy Boys?"

He threw his head back and laughed. "Not even close."

A strong gust of wind blew, and before I could catch my magazine, it fluttered off the table, over the dock, and into the ocean. I groaned. Reading it just wasn't meant to be.

"Whoops," Jack said as we watched the waves carry it away.

"It's okay. I have a chest full of them that I never got around to reading."

His finger went up. "That reminds me—a couple days ago, I found a small chest buried in the garden. I put it in the shed and have been so busy that I never got a chance to take it inside. Walk with me?"

Unnerved and happy to change the subject of Herkimer, I followed him up the grassy incline to the shed.

"So, how are you liking the job?" I asked.

He shrugged. "Normally, can't complain. This morning's 6 a.m. start time hasn't been so swell, though."

"And here I thought I was the only one who had to get up early for the sake of this event." It never ceased to amaze me just how much effort went into these galas.

"Well, lucky for me the other gardener called in yesterday. He came down with a stomach bug, so guess who's pulling a double shift?"

When we reached the shed, Jack opened the doors and reached for a shoebox-sized brown box sitting on a shelf. He wrinkled his nose as he handed it to me. "I tried to brush it off. It looks really old, and the leather was flaking, so I didn't want to do too much damage." He pointed to the brass lock. "Not sure how you guys will open it unless someone has the key."

"Thanks, I'll—"

I was interrupted by a loud clap of thunder. Rain hit the ground in loud rhythmic patters.

"Crap, I should probably go," I said, using my free hand as a poor excuse for a shield from the rain. "Thanks again and good luck today."

With that, I hugged the box to my chest and dashed toward the house.

When I finally reached the covered expanse of the side patio, I stopped to catch my breath. My dress was dripping wet, and my shoes made a sloshing noise with every step. Not wanting to trail water inside, I kicked them off and wrung out my dress. Just before I reached for the doorknob, I paused, a chill going down my spine, and looked over my shoulder.

Standing in the distance and partially hidden by a tree was the old man I'd seen earlier on Main Street, staring back at me. He was dressed in the same clothes he'd worn earlier—I remembered his plaid maroon button down—only now it was soaked and clung to his body.

I opened my mouth to scream, but no sound came out.

Frightened, I charged toward the door, clumsily tripping over my shoes as I threw it open. Then I glanced back in his direction.

There was no one there.

CHAPTER 2

As I stumbled inside the house, a rush of cold air hit me. Teeth chattering, I dashed through the tea room, down the hall, and across the foyer towards the staircase, wanting nothing more than to get out of my wet clothes. But the sight of suitcases being loaded onto a gold dolly stopped me dead in my tracks.

Those weren't mine—my stuff had already been unpacked—which meant that the family must have already arrived. Crap. I bounded up the stairs two at a time, my heart racing.

"MEREDITH!" came a squealing voice.

I didn't have to turn around to know exactly whose voice that was.

"ABBY!" I set the box on a step and dashed back down the stairs, almost getting knocked over by the brunt force of my cousin's hug. "I can't believe you're here, I—"

"Oh, Meredith, keeping quiet about my trip has been so hard! I've known for days that I was coming, but I wanted to surprise you." She was practically jumping up and down, her long, fiery red curls bouncing on her shoulders.

Abby lived in Maine, which meant we didn't see each other nearly as often as we liked. Every summer, Aunt May made it her life's mission to get Abigail to attend etiquette school. And every year, Abigail managed to come up with an excuse. She'd used everything from spearheading a recycling campaign at their local country club to taking horseback lessons—and Abigail hated animals.

"Your dad is a lifesaver," Abby added.

"He talked her out of it again?"

"He sure did! Believe it or not, his campaign is the best excuse mother has heard yet." She held me at arm's length. "Where were you? Rolling around in a mud puddle?"

I swallowed. "Sort of. I mean no . . . I need to talk to you. I think someone—"

"Well, look who's here," came my grandmother's poetic voice from the doorway.

I froze, mortified.

"Grandmother!" Abby exclaimed.

Our grandmother stood rigidly in her sleek brown sheath dress as my cousin wrapped her arms around her. Her gray hair was pinned back in her classic chignon, not a single hair daring to stick out of place. She grimaced as she looked at me, and I internally reprimanded myself for ever going outside.

Shockingly, and surely exercising much restraint, she said nothing about my appearance. Not that she had to. Her expression said it all. Instead, she turned her gaze toward Abby, who was stylishly dressed in black skinny pants, a beige top, and beige heels.

"I've returned to eat lunch with you girls, and then I will be headed back to rejoin Meredith's father." Our grandmother spoke unlike anyone I'd ever heard,

17

enunciating every letter of every word. Not only did it make me want to rip my hair out, but it took insanely long for her to speak. "Come, Abigail, let's go. Edwin must be waiting."

Grandmother raised a commanding eyebrow at me then turned and started walking, her low heels clicking rhythmically on the ancient marble floor.

I quickly scurried up the stairs, grabbing the box along the way, and hastily flung it onto my bed once I reached my room. Then I grabbed the first thing in my closet that I could find, washed the grime off of my arms, legs, and face, and dashed back downstairs to the blue dining room used for lunch. Meals got more elegant as the day wore on; as you could imagine, dinner was quite the production.

At the table beside my grandmother, I saw the back of my grandfather's wheelchair. I slowed to a halt.

"Hello, grandfather," I said as I gently approached him from behind, not wanting to startle him.

For as long as I could remember, my grandfather had been plagued by the effects of a massive stroke that left him wheelchair bound. Since then, his speech had also suffered greatly, and the humiliation he felt at his inability to form recognizable words meant he never dared utter a single syllable. I had no idea what his voice even sounded like.

To my relief, he didn't look much different than the last time I saw him. His sparse white hair was combed to the side and he was clean-shaven, smelling faintly of aftershave. He wore a suit which, given his condition, I thought he filled out just fine. Still, the wrinkles on his face were many, and his bottom lip—much like his eyelids—drooped considerably.

Upon coming into his line of sight, he looked up and gave my hand a loving pat. I took a seat across from my grandparents, next to Abby.

"Laurent has prepared a special meal," grandmother said, feigned excitement in her voice.

Abby and I looked at each other, our eyes widening. What would grandmother's *special meal* consist of this time? Last time we'd summered here, it was chili rubbed ostrich with black bean-corn succotash and ginger-orange syrup. Normally that wouldn't stand out in my mind, but I vividly recall forcing myself not to hurl as I ate, too young at the time to have the courage to ask for something different.

Like clockwork, Laurent and two other helpers brought several serving trays, which they placed in front of us. My forehead creased in apprehension as I waited for them to lift the lids and reveal lunch.

"Spicy tuna in sesame miso cone," he announced as the waiters lifted the silver covers.

"Uh—" I started.

"Is there a problem?" my grandmother asked as she placed a white linen napkin in her lap.

I'd been summering here off and on since I was five, and yet she still didn't get it, no matter how many times I repeated myself. "I'm allergic to fish."

Grandmother raised an eyebrow at the news. "Oh, why yes, that's right." She lifted a finger and another waiter came running. "Bring Meredith something else to eat. The rest of us will eat the tuna."

It was almost humorous to watch her play the role of an amiable hostess when I knew she would rather be drinking tea and eating scones with the area socialites. "I take it you are both looking forward to the gala tonight. Your timing was impeccable, Abigail." She

19

gently lifted a small morsel of tuna to her mouth. Her cheeks moved so subtly that you could hardly even tell she was chewing.

"I am so excited!" Abby said with a squeal.

"Abigail, I know you are excited, but please, dear. You know how rude it is to talk with your mouth full," grandmother said once she had finished her own bite. Then she muttered something about etiquette school under her breath.

"Grandmother," I said in my most serious tone. "I'm afraid there might be someone trying to sabotage father's campaign. On the way from the airport, I saw a protest on Main Street, and then just before lunch, I could swear I saw one of his protesters on the property."

Grandfather raised an eyebrow and slowly turned his head toward my grandmother. Perhaps he hoped for her to speak on his behalf, though she simply looked at me as though I'd gone mad. "Surely you must be mistaken. There are plenty of people on the property today. This event is being catered by the most elite in the business, and that includes our security team. Worry not."

"I know what I saw," I stammered. Although I'd crossed a line that one must never cross with her, oddly enough, I didn't regret it. I would not shy away when my father's safety was involved.

I braced myself for her fire, but shockingly, she simply stood. "There will come a time, young lady, when you will learn to respect your elders. As I said, we've employed the best security in the country. See to it that you are dressed and ready by five." Then she turned on her heels and strode out of the room.

"I hope you're right," I whispered.

With our grandmother safely gone, Abby pushed her plate away. "Well, on the bright side, at least we don't have to eat this crap anymore."

I looked in my grandfather's direction, wondering if he would be mad at her statement, but saw what looked like the beginning of a smile forming on his face.

THE STYLIST, JOE, zipped up the back of my sleeveless navy gown and was fastening a gorgeous diamond necklace around my neck when Abby popped her head into the room. "You ready?"

"Almost—" I started, but the sight of her left me breathless. It wasn't often that I saw my cousin so dressed up. She looked absolutely stunning with her curls carefully pinned back at the nape of her neck. Her natural makeup brought out her emerald eyes. Her floor-length forest green dress looked even brighter when paired with her fiery hair. "You look amazing!"

Her face flushed. "Thanks, it's quite some crew they have here."

I thanked Joe, reached for my clutch, and then Abby and I were on our way. As we descended the grand staircase, I noticed four brawny men strategically placed at every corner of the large room. I let out a breath of relief. Despite my grandmother's reassurance, an uneasy feeling had lingered in my stomach.

"Oh no," Abby said as she looked at the crowd below.

I froze. "What's wrong?"

"That's what's wrong." She pointed to Arthur, who was waiting for us at the bottom of the staircase.

"Homegirls!" he exclaimed, both hands out to high five us. But Abby didn't move a muscle to greet him. Instead, she shot him a murderous look, and I laughed, feeling considerably more at ease now that I realized her concern was completely unwarranted.

"Arthur! Long time no see. How've you been?"

"Keeping out of trouble. Keeping the big guy out of trouble." He gestured towards the campaign picture of my father hanging front and center in the foyer.

"Oh please, you're an *intern*," Abby spewed.

He grinned, puffing his chest. "And the finest one they've had yet."

For whatever reason, his comic worthier-than-thou attitude annoyed Abby to no end. But Arthur was far from cocky. His father had long been my father's chief advisor and was his closest friend since childhood. Although that—and the fact that Arthur just finished his first year at Harvard—meant they were primarily based out of Boston, Arthur grew up in and now summered in Hyannis Port, providing endless opportunities to crash at my grandparents' house— uninvited or not. Growing up, I'd come to look at him as the goofy sibling I only had to put up with during the months of June through August.

"You're looking good," I said, admiring his beige suit and white cotton shirt that was casually unbuttoned under his neck. It was such a quintessential Arthur look—casual enough that he could go from party to perfunctory in no time.

He ran a hand over his slicked back brown hair and shrugged. "You know, gotta maintain my image." He winked, and I would have bet the dress off my back that Abby was rolling her eyes.

I was just about to reply when the room went dead silent.

I followed the direction of the turning heads to see my grandmother standing in the doorway wearing an elegant black gown with a matching cropped jacket. That explained the silence. Around her neck was a lavish diamond necklace that sparkled even from where I stood. Much like the Queen of England, for a few long moments she simply stood, gauging the appearances of each member of her family. Should anything be amiss, a grimace would have been clearly visible on her face. If something was terribly amiss, she would surely comment. This time, however, she pursed her lips and took a step forward while the entire room let out a collective sigh of relief.

After greetings were exchanged, grandmother gestured toward the doorway of the ballroom. "Let us proceed inside," she said as she turned and led the way.

China and stemware lined the crisp white tables. Elaborate centerpieces overflowing with bouquets from grandmother's garden filled the air with the sweet smell of peonies and tulips. At the head of the ballroom, a podium had been erected for my father's speech, a garland with his campaign picture and title matching the others that decorated the walls of the large space.

We all gathered at the prime front row tables reserved for family and sat while grandmother made her way back to the door to greet the many guests that were arriving. From experience, I knew grandfather preferred not to make appearances at such big events, and I couldn't say that I blamed him. Pity was a natural reaction to his plight. Besides, not being able to speak made being cordial quite a challenge. Luckily for him, my grandmother lacked no social graces.

A short while later, white-gloved staff began to serve hors d'oeuvres and cocktails to the adults, sparkling cider for Abigail and myself. Apart from the subtle clink of silverware, my family noshed in silence as they awaited the start of the program.

My uncle Ephraim cleared his throat. "Where's Magnus?" Uncle E had a strong jaw and brooding appearance although there wasn't a sweeter man in existence. His hair was dark like mine, but his eyes were a light greenish-grey. He and his wife Sarah had two children, Madeleine and Nadine.

"Giving a last minute interview," uncle Charlie replied. He looked a lot more like grandfather with a round face, thick hair, and dark brown eyes.

Nearly an hour later, most of the guests were settled in. The side door eventually opened, and my father stepped into the arena to the sound of applause. He was dressed in a sharp navy blue suit, his salt and pepper colored hair combed to the side.

He ascended the three stairs on the side of the stage and stood at the podium for several long moments before beginning his introduction. "It is an honor and a privilege to have you here this evening. This event is one of the most important ones I will attend in my campaign for governor of the great state of Massachusetts. I am excited to be able to count on your support."

My family clapped and I methodically emulated their motions. Truth be told, I wasn't sure how I felt about my father's candidacy.

"I am wholly committed to representing the people's voice—your voice—and bringing our concerns to Washington to be heard and acted upon—"

I'd heard this pitch more times than I liked to count. I leaned in towards Abby. "Want to bail after dinner?"

"It can't come soon enough," she replied.

Not wanting to appear disrespectful, I directed my attention back to my father. " . . . campaign has come to mean a great deal to me."

But it was only more of the same.

SEVERAL HOURS LATER, after sitting through what felt like endless back-to-back dinner courses and dessert, Abby and I were spent. My father was still going strong, strategically moving from table to table to chat with his constituents. Now, he took to the stage once more. "I sincerely hope you've enjoyed this lovely meal. Thank you for your generous contributions tonight. I now invite you to put on your dancing shoes and join us on the dance floor."

In the corner of the ballroom, the live orchestra was getting ready to begin.

I glanced at Abby, "Ready?"

She nodded, and we stood.

When we reached the door, a loud muffled sound filled the room, sending us to a skidding halt. A voice replaced what should have been music, and it only took me a few seconds to realize whose voice it was.

"I took care of her, she will never see the light of day again," my father said in what was clearly a recording. Although it was slightly muffled, what he said next left no room for misinterpretation. "Money always wins. It has since the beginning of time. I can assure you, with enough incentive, the jury's vote is all ours. She's done for."

Shocked at his words, I glared at my father, who stood taken aback on the stage.

"Cut the tape," he demanded, all eyes now on him. "It's a setup!"

The security guards I had been so happy to see earlier now swarmed around the DJ's station. What happened next was nothing short of organized chaos. Angry partygoers abruptly stood, and the room came alive with chatter. Blinding camera flashes burst at every angle as the paid photographers morphed from loyal endorsers to hounding paparazzi faster than the split-second shutter time on their cameras. For several long moments, my father simply glanced from one end of the room to the other, looking desperate. Then he stood up straight and moved closer to the podium.

"Rest assured that recording is not as cryptic as it sounded," he began, even mustering a fake-sounding chuckle. But that didn't stop people from leaving.

He went on to explain that the "her" he referred to was apparently an ex-staff member who stole confidential client files from his law firm many years back. She was imprisoned for that and various other charges, thus his reference to her never seeing the light of day. The story sounded plausible enough, but something about his tone in the recording still made me feel as though the story didn't entirely add up.

AN HOUR LATER, Abby and I staggered upstairs to my bedroom, leaving my father to make the final farewell rounds to the few remaining guests.

I flicked on the light in my room and kicked off my heels, Abby following suit, exhausted after having started my day so early.

"The press is going to be *all* over this," I said. I was just about to collapse onto my bed, formal dress and all, when I noticed the box the gardener had given me earlier sitting atop my comforter.

"Uncle Magnus can handle it. He will obviously have to do damage control, but he'll overcome this." She sat down beside me and looked at the box. "What's that?"

I explained where it had come from, to which she replied, "You really think you're going to be able to hand grandmother a box that's been covered in dirt for God knows how long and not expect her to have the staff throw it straight into the garbage?"

"You're right," I replied, reaching for it. As the gardener had pointed out, the leather was flaking in parts, but the brass handle and metal stud decorations were intact. I turned it around, looking at the sides. On the right were the letters RC, the year 1885 on the left.

"That's over a hundred years old!" Abby exclaimed, moving closer to look at the details.

"RC," I read. "The house was built by an Abraham Cabot sometime in the late 1800s—you can thank one boring afternoon in grandfather's library for how I know that—maybe it belonged to a member of his family?"

"Whatever, you've always had a knack for history. Do you know what year exactly it was built?"

"No, but it shouldn't be too hard to find out," I replied.

"Well, what are you waiting for, open it!"

I looked at Abby in surprise. "You really think grandmother won't want it?"

Her eyebrows creased inwards. "You do realize who you're talking about, don't you?"

Despite the stress of the evening, I chuckled, my grandmother's reaction playing out in my head. The box was secured by a rusted lock, which, from the look of it, didn't seem too difficult to break. I got up and fished around in the desk drawer for scissors. After several forceful attempts to pry the bolt, the lock cracked, and the box flew open out of my grasp and landed on my bed, its contents strewn about.

My eyes widened, and I gasped. On the bedspread lay at least a dozen pieces of glittering diamond and gemstone jewels.

And a gun.

## CHAPTER 3

The morning after the gala, I awoke to sunlight hitting my face and birds chirping outside my window. For the briefest moment, I almost forgot how gloomy yesterday was. This looked more like the summers that I remembered. Figures that I would be leaving just as the weather turned pleasant.

Beside me, Abigail stirred and rubbed her eyes. "Sleep well?"

For a few long seconds, I stayed quiet, groggy and trying to put together the random pieces of the night before.

"I tossed and turned a lot," I replied. And it was no wonder. Last night we'd marveled over the box's contents. Sets of antique necklaces and earrings, bracelets and rings. All were beyond exquisite and, even more important, authentic. And that gun. Too scared to know what to do with it, we'd hidden it in the bottommost drawer of the nightstand. I reached over and opened it.

"Still exactly where we left it," I said and closed the drawer.

The idea of having a gun in my room unnerved me, but we'd both agreed that telling grandmother last night was not the right time, especially after my father's little blunder.

"That R. Cabot has some explaining to do," Abby had said as we tried on and modeled the jewels in our evening gowns. "This jewelry has to be worth a small fortune. And I don't even want to think about why there's a gun in the mix."

I shook away the memory from last night just as there was a quiet knock at my door.

"Come in," I called, propping myself up in bed.

Tillie stepped inside, her light brown hair pinned up in a bun, her pale blue uniform and white apron freshly pressed. "Madam Worthington would like you to join her in the tearoom."

Tillie curtsied and left the room. Her movements were so robotic, as though she had been trained exactly how to behave. I couldn't help but pity her—and all of the staff for that matter. Was she married? Did she have a family of her own? And how was it that she didn't throw in the towel after spending so much time and effort waiting on my grandparents' every whim?

After slipping our robes on and washing up, Abigail and I got dressed for the day and went downstairs. Already seated around the breakfast table in the forest-green colored room was our family. Miraculously, even my father was there.

"Good morning," I said as we hurried to our seats.

Grandmother rang the small porcelain bell to signal the staff to bring our food.

Everything was done in such a hurry. Once one plate was set down, there was another right behind it. My stomach growled loudly at the fresh fruit, omelets, and croissants, startling me so that I jumped up in my chair, my hand knocking the silverware on the table.

Everyone turned to me. Embarrassed, I hunched over and held my stomach tight.

Breakfast, like every other meal, was eaten in relative silence, because God forbid someone spoke with food in their mouth. With my father's somber mood this morning, though, it was probably a blessing in disguise. By the time I finished with my eggs and croissant with grape jelly, everyone else was still just beginning. I sat back and waited, watching everybody eat. I watched as uncle Ephraim leisurely lifted a small morsel of omelet to his mouth, promptly closing and chewing slowly—if he continued at this pace, we would be here until tomorrow morning. My grandmother sipped her tea while Abigail opted for a second croissant.

After what seemed like an eternity later, grandmother rang the bell again; the sight of dirty dishes made her cringe. In the past, I'd fantasized about telling her to clean them up herself, imagining myself boldly standing up and telling her to simply get over it. If only I was that brave.

"I take it everyone has enjoyed their stay," she said once the table had been cleared.

"It's been a pleasure, as always," uncle Charlie said, wiping his mouth with a white linen napkin.

She gave him a subtle smile, then turned to my father. "Magnus, there's something I'd like to propose."

My father looked up from the morning paper—his face, as expected, was splashed on the cover. "Yes, mother?"

"I'd like to have Meredith stay with us this summer."

If I'd had food in my mouth I probably would have choked.

31

"You are going to be busy with your campaign, and a summer here is exactly what she needs. Why, even Abigail's mother has decided to allow her to forego her summer plans to stay. Surely you'll see the value and guidance I can provide to these two young ladies."

Abby, who had been sipping her orange juice, really did choke.

"See," grandmother said, gesturing at my gasping cousin. "It's a fine idea if I ever did have one."

My father looked at me. "I leave the decision to you."

"Abby is going to stay?" I asked warily. Although staying at Greyhurst was not what I had in mind, in some ways it sounded better than going back to the advanced biology and chemistry classes I'd signed up for at my boarding school's summer program. Would I rather spend my summer pouring over books or teacups?

Abby's hand reached for mine, and she gave me a squeeze. "Don't you dare leave me alone," she whispered.

I couldn't leave Abby even if the idea of staying at Greyhurst felt like someone hammering nails into my skull. I tried to see a bright side—it *had* been a while since the two of us summered together. For some reason, I also thought of the box sitting in my nightstand. Maybe a summer here really could be interesting. My father would be busier than I was used to, if that was even possible. Plus, I wasn't exactly looking forward to flying again so soon. I gulped.

"Sure . . . thank you for the invitation, grandmother."

Satisfied, she sipped her tea.

And, just like that, my fate was sealed.

32

AFTER BIDDING MY father and uncles goodbye, Abigail and I reconvened in my bedroom to decide our afternoon plans. Grandmother had a social event to attend, grandfather still hadn't woken up, and the staff was busy tidying up after yesterday's gala, so the day was pretty much ours.

"I don't know about you, but I am dying to lay out by the beach and take a dip. I really need to unwind after finals." Not to mention my skin had taken on a ghostly pallor after being holed up studying all the time. I looked at her with a smirk, knowing exactly what she would say.

Abigail's hatred of animals included fish. Especially fish. Petrified of what lurked below, Abby refused to go into any water that she could not see through.

"Fine by me," she stated matter-of-factly.

I put my hand to her forehead and feigned panic. "Are you feeling okay?"

"I didn't say I was going *into* the water, but I would like to lay out *by* the water and tan. You, my dear, are swimming alone."

I opened the closet and rifled through the items Tillie had unpacked, trying to find my swimsuit and cover up. Despite the short time I'd have here, the pool was definitely worth visiting so I'd come prepared. Soon I'd have the rest of my wardrobe to choose from; after accepting her invitation, my grandmother promptly ordered the staff to have both mine and Abigail's belongings flown in.

"I'm sure grandmother's got some ancient swim suit you could borrow. You can call it vintage," Abby said as she sauntered out of my room.

"Funny," I said, pulling out my black two-piece suit and sundress. Abigail returned a few minutes later, donning a bright multicolored maxi dress, her wild red curls lying loose on her shoulders.

Once seaside, Abby arranged our belongings on the table, and after applying sunscreen, retreated to the lounge chairs where she lied down to sunbathe.

The ocean spanned as far as my eyes could see. The sunlight sparkled off the deep blue sea like glitter dancing on a sapphire waterbed. Around us, seagulls bobbed in the water or flew overhead. Even the Herkimer mansion didn't look so ominous today.

Eager to get into the water, I slipped out of my dress and took off toward the waves.

The feeling of the cool water on my dry, warm skin felt like a thousand little needles. I wiped the water off my face and pulled the hair tie out of my limp ponytail, throwing it in Abigail's direction on the sand.

"You don't know what you're missing," I yelled to her.

"You have fun out there!"

The further out I swam, the more the rays of the sun warmed my skin. I closed my eyes and let myself completely unwind, my arms and legs lying limply against the surface of the waves as I savored the tranquility.

I drifted for what seemed like an eternity until the sun became obscured by passing clouds and the water turned cooler. Shivering from the cool breeze blowing in off the shore, I scurried to where Abby sat, wrapped myself in a towel, and silently begged the sun to return.

"Well, don't you two look comfortable."

I turned around to see Arthur in swim shorts, a towel draped over his shoulder, walking toward us.

"Please tell me I'm having a nightmare," Abby said, not opening an eye.

"Try to contain your joy," he said as he plopped himself down next to us. "Word on the street is that you two found yourselves a home for the summer. I've actually come to relieve you both of your boredom. I figure somebody has to show you a good time."

"Not interested," Abby spat. "Don't you have work to do? It's certainly a convenient time to be on vacation given that uncle Magnus needs all the help he can get."

"You know you might want to flip over, unless flamingo is trending this summer."

Abby bolted upright and looked at her bright pink legs.

"Crap," she said, pulling a towel over her skin.

I pulled a towel around my shoulders and peered up at Arthur. "So how exactly do you plan on entertaining us?"

"By taking you out for a spin on my boat. Did you think I really *walked* all the way from our house?"

"Don't act so high and mighty," Abby spewed.

Then a fourth voice popped into our conversation. "Mind if I crash your get-together?"

I looked over my shoulder to see Jack. "Actually, your timing couldn't be better," I said. "These two are at each other's throats—long story."

He smiled, revealing dimples that I hadn't noticed yesterday. Today he wore a V-neck T-shirt, heavy Caterpillar boots, and khaki cargo shorts that revealed his toned leg muscles.

"I was just about to take these two out for a boat ride," Arthur said. "You're welcome to come."

I frowned, picking up on a hint of familiarity in Arthur's tone. "Do you two know each other?"

"Your grandmother loaned Jack out to help my mother earlier this week," Arthur said. "I've been filling him in on the ins and outs of Harvard."

"I see."

Arthur stood. "So what do you say about an impromptu boat ride."

"I'm out. I don't do boats. Have fun, Meredith," Abigail said. "I think I'm going to jump in the pool. I'm feeling a little warm." She touched her arms; her skin turned white from the pressure and immediately returned to a bright shade of pink. Someone was sure going to be sore tonight . . .

"I'll drive over to the dock. I'd hate to make you guys *walk*," Arthur spoke in Abby's direction as he started off down the shoreline.

"Have fun," Abby said as she went in the complete opposite direction.

Jack rolled forward on his toes. "I don't know what it is, but something tells me those two get along just fine."

I chuckled, then slipped my dress back on over my bathing suit. "Is it that obvious?"

He put his hands in his pockets and tilted his head toward the dock. "Shall we?"

"Sure," I replied as we began to walk.

"So, have an interesting night last night?" he asked.

At first I thought he was referring to the chest he'd given me but realized that wasn't all that happened. "I take it you've seen the news."

He hesitated. "I have . . . but I wouldn't worry about it. More scandalous things have been leaked about candidates that haven't put a dent in their campaigns. This too shall pass."

"I suppose you're right."

"Will you be staying the summer?"

"I will now . . . Before this morning, I was counting the hours until I left back to New Hampshire. My boarding school has a five-week summer program that I decided to take when my dad announced his campaign. I figured I'd try to stay out of his hair without dying of boredom. I wasn't exactly thrilled at the idea of spending my time off taking three courses plus athletics but whatever . . . I won't have to worry about it now that my grandmother offered to have Abby and I stay the summer."

He raised his eyebrows. "Boarding school, huh? Do you have any siblings? I can't imagine what your mom does all day while you're away and your dad's campaigning."

I stiffened, bracing myself for the dreaded mother conversation that always seemed to come up with people I didn't know.

"I'm an only child. My mother pretty much birthed me and bailed." The words sounded cold, but after all these years, I couldn't find it in me to have any remorse.

My mother had chosen to turn her back on us, I'd merely come to accept it like it was. Still, I didn't go into details about how I really felt; I never told anyone how my father still hadn't gotten over her, that the only reason I put up with this campaign and all his other business endeavors that had left him absent was because busying himself was the only way he knew how to cope. I spared people the true reality that my father was a broken man, a far cry from the powerful, smiling person who came across on all the posters. And I would never, ever tell anyone that there was another reason he was always gone: because the mere sight of me, the daughter who was a spitting image of her mother, pained him to his core.

Jack stopped just short of the dock. "I'm sorry. I honestly didn't—"

"No, no," I reassured him. "Talking about it doesn't faze me anymore. I can't mourn the absence of someone I don't even remember." A seagull flew overhead, squawked, and planted one right in front of where we stood. "See," I said, laughing. "Someone is in agreement."

"So you can call this a pathetic attempt to change the subject, but would you believe me if I told you that I'd never seen a seagull before I came here?"

My eyes widened. "How is that possible?"

"Well, for starters, I never left my hometown before coming here. Which, yes, means that I'd never ridden on an airplane."

My mouth fell open. "I guess seagulls wouldn't exactly thrive in Canada. Was it really cold where you lived?"

He chuckled. "Cold. Dismal. Non-existent light in the winter, never ending sunlight in the summer. I think that sums it up nicely."

"With a pitch like that, it's a shame the tourist bureau doesn't hire you for campaigns."

He laughed. "Oh that's just the start, I could go on and on about having to walk home from school in the freezing rain. My friends and I kept a running count of who wound up with hypothermia the most."

I stared at him, incredulous. "Because that's something to be proud of . . . ?"

"Why, of course. Our reputations were built on who was dumb enough to test fate." He laughed. "Johnny Brighton took the crown with seven. I made it to three. First time at age ten . . . I fell in a ditch. The other two times were completely my fault. I was a pretty rambunctious boy; my mom couldn't keep me indoors if she tied me to a chair. But on the bright side, I got a cell phone out of it."

"Ah, the silver lining."

The sound of an engine approaching signaled Arthur's return. "Seriously, you two, I can't get it any closer. Let's go."

Jack and I exchanged grins and proceeded down the dock.

He jumped first, rocking the boat as he landed full center. The water around the boat rippled, sending symmetrical rings cascading away until they finally dissipated. He put a hand out to help me. Nervous that I wouldn't be as adept, I accepted and stepped onto the edge, immediately slipping on the wet surface and tumbling into the boat.

"Whoa! Careful. I don't have my first aid kit on me this time," he joked as he helped me up. "You okay?"

"I'm fine," I said as I steadied myself. Way to keep it graceful.

Jack and I each took one of the seats on either side of the boat while Arthur revved up the engine. "Welcome aboard the King Arthur."

And with that, we were off.

The wind violently whipped my hair as Arthur led us along the coastline. The dock was now in the distance, but from where we sat so far away, we could still see Greyhurst looming large. We were also offered a prime view of the other water-front mansions— Arthur's family's included—that, like Greyhurst, were hidden among the trees of the main road, invisible to any passersby. I'd never been out on boat here; clearly my grandparents weren't the nautical type. A ride like this would probably make grandmother keel over . . . and grandfather? Surely he would have a second stroke. But I liked to imagine that, in their youth, they'd had an adventurous spirit. Life was too short to spend it looking as though you'd been sucking on a lemon.

Eventually, Arthur cut the engine and we sat suspended in the center of the sea. I savored the sun's rays beaming down on my skin, soaking up the sound of the blue water and the sight of the lush greenery on the shore in the distance. "This is really great, Arthur, thanks."

But he and Jack were busy looking at the fish finder.

"Hey, Mere, what do you say we take a snapshot of this and frame it for Abby," Arthur said.

In spite of my efforts not to, I couldn't help but laugh. "She'd kill you."

Arthur and Jack started talking boat lingo, a subject I knew absolutely nothing about, so I went back to my reverie. My eyes settled on the Herkimer island, which was now visible in much more detail. The house was clearly Victorian, with a grey exterior, tall mansard roof, and giant cupola, and was so large it almost looked like a castle. A long porch wrapped around the exterior accented by intricate carvings, which gave the mansion an almost Gothic aura. Oddly, the details I was seeing for the first time in person were almost exactly what I recalled from my dreams.

"Hey, what do you say we pull up close and check out Herkimer?" I asked, surprising even myself. After all, only yesterday I'd lectured Jack on having no desire to tempt the curse that so many believed lingered within its walls.

Jack raised an eyebrow while Arthur appeared hesitant.

"Uh, you sure?" Arthur said.

"Dude, who spayed you? Don't tell me you think it's cursed, too," Jack said. "What is it with you people?"

What he said must have had serious meaning in man-code, because Arthur sat up straight as an arrow, powered the boat on, and said, "You're right, let's go."

## CHAPTER 4

Arthur veered the boat up to the tattered old dock connected to the large boathouse at the foot of the island. Seeing it up close for the first time, I marveled at how enormous Herkimer really was—and that was what was still standing. Three floors loomed before us, an elegant tower-like structure crowning the top of the mansion. Several stained glass windows accented the exterior, and the intricate patterns in the brickwork were apparent even from here. Time and the fire had taken its toll, but from what was left, it was obvious this had been quite a house. That poor woman who never got to see the surprise her husband had in store for her.

The engine cut abruptly, and Jack graciously offered to help Arthur anchor the boat, hoisting himself up to receive the rope. The dock creaked under his weight as he secured it to the warped wooden post.

"Be careful," I said, suddenly a little apprehensive. Not only were we trespassing, which was a big enough offense, but the property had been condemned.

Once anchored, Arthur climbed up to the dock, and together they tested their weight on various points before Jack came back and offered a hand. "It seems alright. I'll go first, and you can retrace my steps."

The turbulent wind on the island blew my hair about, whipping me in the face as I carefully maneuvered the boards, following his footwork exactly. In the distance a flagpole rattled as the torn fabric twisted violently in the wind. Although the sun shone brightly, I shivered.

"Ready?" Arthur asked once we were safely on solid ground.

"Let's do it," I said.

We made our way up the incline through the untrimmed grass and overgrown weeds until we reached a moss-covered clearing. Through the matted green growth, I could vaguely make out dark grey concrete and realized that we were now on a sidewalk. My eyes followed the winding path that led straight to the entrance.

A gorgeous wraparound porch hugged the exterior of the house, and the iron rails twisted into an elegant spindle-like shape that, like the rest of the house, was covered in decades worth of untouched ivy. Large cement columns lined the veranda and broken windows framed the house. As we ascended the ancient steps, I looked around the porch. Two tattered wooden rocking chairs sat on either side of a table, one upright and the other laying on its side. On the table lay two facedown dolls surrounded by shards of flower-adorned, cream-colored glass. Intrigued, I took one in my hand, turning it over. A scream wedged in my throat. The inked details of the doll's face were gone. An eyeless, featureless porcelain canvas remained.

"Now that's freaky," Arthur said with a shudder.

I nodded. Somehow, the longer I looked at it, the more I could see past the faceless exterior. I stroked the doll's long brown hair, trying to remove the bits of leaves and dirt caught in it. Finally, I straightened its dress and matching apron, which were now nearly colorless from exposure to the elements, and returned it to the table. Then something dawned on me.

"That's strange," I said aloud.

"Yeah, I'd say so," Arthur said.

"It's not just the doll . . . The story about this place—they said no one's ever lived here."

Arthur shrugged. To my left, Jack walked up to peer into one of the windows. At first he simply looked, then he cupped his hands around his eyes to block out the sunlight.

"See anything?" I asked.

"It's too dark. I think I see the silhouette of a hutch, or maybe it's a fireplace." He withdrew himself from the glass and turned around to look at me.

I couldn't help but chuckle.

"What?"

"Your nose . . . and forehead," I said between giggles. "They are covered in soot."

He swiped his hand over his forehead, producing filth on his fingers. "Awesome."

"You're making it worse. Come here." I wiped the grime away as best as I could manage without water, trying to scrub it away with my clean fingers.

"Thanks," he said with a generous smile.

Arthur reached out to test the doorknob, which surprisingly turned without any resistance.

"A tell-tale sign that the world was once a much safer place," I marveled.

I stepped inside behind him, the light suddenly fading into almost complete darkness. Instantly, my eyes stung from the thick, musty air, and my lungs felt more and more constricted with each breath. Jack and Arthur coughed.

Once my eyes adjusted to the dark, I took in the area. Old Victorian furniture and English tapestries furnished the space, which looked as though it had been well-preserved under the layer of black ash. A tall grandfather clock loomed in the hallway, the minute and hour hands frozen at a little over half past three. Mirrors—or were they paintings?—hung on the wall in a perfect perpendicular manner and were topped with white sheets. Residue-covered belongings coated the floor and the long winding wooden staircase off to the right. I paused to look at the old-fashioned sewing machine and oil lamp, which sat atop a nearby table.

My grandparents had their fair share of collectables and antiques, but still I had never seen anything like this.

"This place is unreal," Jack said in awe, his voice barely a whisper. He was bent over an aged chest sitting near the fireplace.

I approached a desk perched in the corner of the room, atop which sat an old phonograph. Ever so carefully, I lifted the needle onto the dusty record, but nothing happened.

"You guys, over here," Arthur called out excitedly.

I followed his voice through the dark halls to an adjacent room. A large canopy bed took up the center of the space. The bed frame was crafted of heavy dark wood of which the matching chair and footstool were also made. Next to the bed was a side table, a stack of dusty, leather-bound books and a bronze reading lamp on its surface.

I ran my hand along the bedspread. Velvet. Tassels and ruffles accented the corners of the duvet that, in the dim light, I presumed to be either maroon or purple. Matching floral draperies framed the single large window. Above the bed hung an ornate oil painting depicting a field of flowers.

I pulled the sheet off the mirror on the vanity to reveal intricately carved wood that was now covered in dust and cobwebs. On the surface of the table was an antique silver tray embellished with detailed filigree cutouts and three elaborate perfume bottles.

"I can't get over this place," I exclaimed, my mouth agape.

"Wait till you get a load of this." Arthur looked mesmerized as he stared into an external wardrobe.

I proceeded to his side and gasped. Inside the wardrobe hung a row of beautiful Victorian gowns. I immediately reached out to touch one of the dated dresses, marveling at the discovery.

"That story is so wrong," I said as I scooped one of the dresses off the oddly shaped hanger and laid it out on the bed. "Somebody definitely lived here!"

The dress was heavy, and I had to use both hands to straighten it. How on earth did women wear these? The luxurious gown was made out of rich jewel-tone fabrics affixed with everything from lace to expertly placed beads. A high collar and puffed sleeves accented the bodice of the dress. I was in awe. Even my grandmother had never scored such artifacts.

"It doesn't make sense," Arthur whispered.

Beside me, Jack also stared at the garments. "This place is like a museum frozen in time."

I walked over to the vanity and opened the top drawer only to find it filled with linens. The second drawer was no different. I was about to move on to the third when I noticed that amongst the white fabric was a faint silhouette of something dark. I frowned. I had almost missed it, being that it was hard to see with the faint trace of sunlight peering through the ash-covered window, but there was something there.

I ran my hand through the linens and produced a small, leather-bound book. Carefully, I flipped through the delicate, lightly penned, cursive-filled pages and walked over to the window to make out the text more clearly.

The first entry was dated Monday, January 21st, 1888. Awestruck, I began to read.

*Henry is unwell; Master Walter set out to fetch for the doctor, and we all sit anxious for his return. I reckon that without haste, poor Henry will not survive. Of my many prayers is that Royce never cease to remain in good health. No longer does he finish his porridge, and I fret for his slight frame. I must summon the courage to ask Madam Rowena for milk. Perhaps after Henry becomes well.*

*I write today breathless from the cold and stormy weather. My limbs scream from the frigid temperatures. Word of blizzards past abounds, but none could possibly compare with this fiendish onslaught. The demands of Madam Rowena multiply with the cold, and I find myself unable to spare more than a few moments time to write this account. I must return to my work; Madam Rowena has requested that I repolish the silver. My only consolation is that it places me near the fireplace for a few precious moments.*

*God's faithful servant,*
*Josephine*

Reluctantly, I closed the book after reading the first entry, but desperately wanted nothing more than to sit and read the diary cover to cover. It was fascinating.

Did Henry survive? Without thinking twice, I tucked the journal under my arm.

"Stealing, are we?" Arthur asked as he plucked the book from my hold.

I pulled it out of his hands. "No, not stealing, borrowing. I'll put it back once I read through."

"I think it could be interesting," Jack volunteered. He was crouched on the ground, looking through a small chest. "Plus it's not like anyone would know it's missing."

"Whatever you say, Sherlock. I'm going to look around," Arthur said as he strode out of the room.

Although I too was intrigued by what else there was to see in the house, there was still so much to comb through in the living room and bedroom alone, and I wanted to take my time.

"I wish it wasn't so hard to get here . . . I would love to spend my summer exploring this place. Abby doesn't know what she's missing," I said to Jack as I thought of my cousin who was probably lying poolside, oblivious to the treasure we had stumbled upon.

"I'm really surprised a historical society hasn't gotten its hands on this place," Jack said.

That reminded me. "Hey, remember that box that you gave me?"

He looked at me sideways. "Yeah."

I glanced around the room. "Well, to be honest . . . I didn't exactly give it to my grandmother."

"Oh," he said.

"I knew she wouldn't appreciate it for what it was, she'd probably just have thrown it out unopened. Anyways, Abby and I looked inside and you'll never guess what we found!"

He raised his eyebrows.

"Jewels—it was full of them. And I'm not talking fake costume jewelry. I'm talking Queen Elizabeth-like jewels. And that's all. There was a gun."

He frowned. "A gun?"

"Not like a gun you'd see today. I guess you could call it a pistol, if that's even the right description."

"So you're telling me there was a box full of real jewels—and a pistol—buried in the garden? Why wouldn't they be, I don't know, in a bank or something?"

"You would think they would be. But I have a theory. I think the very first owners of the house put them there for some reason, maybe they were trying to hide them and never made it back to get them."

Shrugging, he said, "You know, I'm really glad you stayed the summer. Something tells me it could get interesting."

HALF AN HOUR later, after Jack and I had combed through the antiquated machines and fixtures in the living room, he said, "I think I'm going to head outside for some fresh air. Should we get Arthur?"

"Fresh air sounds like a good idea. I'm getting a headache. But we can give Arthur a few more minutes; I'm sure he'll come find us when he's ready."

Jack and I stepped outside, and what a difference it made. My lungs felt like sponges in a puddle and happily soaked in the fresh air, although my eyes stung from the sunlight.

"While we wait, how about we check around back," I suggested, wanting to get a good look at the effects of the fire.

I set the diary on the porch table where the creepy dolls lay and started around the right side of the property, which was the only side of the house that didn't have a porch or patio. The grass was overgrown so much that I spent most of my time looking down, scared of snakes or other rodents that had probably found an undisturbed home here.

Jack seemed to do the same, eventually stopping and reaching down to pick something up.

"A bell," he said as he toyed with it.

"Interesting," I mused. It was small and rusted, but worked perfectly as Jack shook it.

He shrugged and tossed it back in the grass where it landed with a muted clamor.

I continued a few steps, still looking down, and frowned. In the grass was yet another bell, identical to the one Jack had just held.

"There's another one," I said.

"Maybe they grazed cows over here. It's not like they could easily get to the supermarket . . . "

That made sense. I pointed a few feet away. "There must have been quite a few."

He grinned. "I don't believe cows practiced celibacy, even if they were in a pretty strict era."

"Funny," I chided, throwing the bell back into the grass and continuing my trek towards the back of the house. Unlike the front, the back was nothing short of an eyesore with shattered windows, blackened walls, and broken shingles.

Jack put a hand out to stop my next step. "I'd be careful. You're wearing sandals, and there could be glass."

I stopped; there really wasn't much to see amongst the ash. "You're right, it's not worth getting stitches."

We reached the front just as Arthur was hurriedly descending the porch stairs two at a time. "I think we should head back. Let's go." Arthur's forehead was damp with sweat and he spoke rapidly. Something about him was definitely off, and I looked up at Jack, wondering if he noticed, too.

"Are you all right?" I asked, practically jogging to catch up with Arthur, who was halfway back to the boat already.

He nodded but didn't stop. "I'm fine."

But I knew that was a lie.


"HAVE FUN?" ABBY asked when I appeared in the doorway of her room after having searched for her by the pool. She was lying atop her comforter on her back with nothing but a towel draped over her for privacy, her sunburned arms and legs sticking straight out at her sides.

I entered cautiously. "Are you okay?"

She didn't move. "I just sponged milk all over my skin. I Googled sunburn remedies."

I spotted a glass and washcloth on the nightstand and wrinkled my nose. But I didn't say anything. "I wish you had come with us. It was amazing."

I sat down in the armchair next to her bed and proceeded to fill her in on our findings, going into great detail on everything from the dresses to the dolls. Then I paused.

"Damn it!" I said suddenly.

"What?"

I explained the diary I found and the passage I'd read. "I forgot it outside on the porch table. I'm so mad!"

"You can always go back and get it," she suggested, lying so still that it kind of felt like I was talking to someone in a coma.

Miffed, I replied, "Do you know how hard it is to get there? Where would I even get a boat if it wasn't for Arthur's?"

"Oh, come on, it can't be that bad."

"Like you would know," I muttered under my breath. Then I stood up. "I'll let you, uh, do whatever it is that you're doing. Find me when you're done?"

"You bet," she replied, her eyes closed.

LATER THAT NIGHT, I awoke without reason. On my lap was a novel I'd tried to read but couldn't get into, the small flashlight I'd used to see it still shining dimly as it lost power. I powered it off, then put the book on my nightstand, struggling to remember the last time I'd woken up so suddenly, so wide awake.

Abby and I had spent a good part of the evening looking online for information about Greyhurst, trying to find out more about the elusive RC. Multiple websites confirmed that Greyhurst was in fact built in 1876 and belonged to the Cabots until 1958 when my family acquired the property. From the looks of it, it seemed quite plausible from the RC inscription and year 1885 that the box—and its contents—belonged to a member of Abraham Cabot's family. Now we would just have to figure out whom. From what we could deduce without combing too much through convoluted family trees, there were multiple members of the family whose names began with R: Robert, Ruth, Ray, Rebecca. At least we now had grounds to start more research.

Sighing and very much frustrated and annoyed that the clock on my nightstand said 2:27 a.m., I got up out of bed. On my way to the bathroom, I paused to look out my window at the tranquil landscape below lit by the white glow of the garden lights. It was beautiful at night, the way the contrast of light and dark played on each other. But the beams strained my eyes, so I directed my gaze toward the blackness of the ocean. I scanned the panorama, making out the faint silhouette of Herkimer and recalling our earlier adventure. Then I did a double take at what I saw, sure my eyes were fooling me.

Faintly illuminated in the mansion's windows was light.

CHAPTER 5

With my father gone, our grandmother made it her sole purpose to see that Abigail and I received a lesson in etiquette like no other. "I certainly cannot return you the way you came or what good will your stay have been?" she'd said Monday over brunch. As a result, the week had been spent learning the do's and don'ts of dining, guidelines for appropriate table conversation, manners in public places, and social meet and greet guidelines. Not only did my back ache from all the posture adjustments, but in our days shadowing her every move, she'd also succeeded in instilling a lifetime hatred of tea, the morning paper, and the violin—turns out my fingers were too short for the piano.

Our first respite came on Friday when a local country club social engagement promised to keep her out of our hair for the day. Knowing she was gone, I happily silenced my alarm when it went off at eight, waking again just shy of noon when my cell phone rang.

As I sat up in bed, my body begging me for a few more moments to wake up, the voicemail alert sounded, and I saw that I'd just missed a call from my father. Instead of listening to the message, I immediately called him back and greeted him groggily.

"Did I wake you?" he asked, remorse coating his voice.

"No, no. I was just getting up. Today's the first day grandmother didn't have us up and at it," I said, trying to sound more alert.

"Are you having a nice time? You can come home anytime, you know."

"It's been great," I replied, surprised that I really didn't want to go anywhere just yet. "How's everything going? You sound a little tired yourself."

He sighed. "It's been busy. Back to back appearances and constant consultations with the team after that little hiccup. We're in Springfield now. There's a rally tonight."

"Did the fundraiser do well given the circumstances?"

"We managed to meet our goal, yes, even after some withdrew their pledges. I'm not sure if you've seen it yet, but my first TV commercial aired yesterday."

"That's great!" I said, meaning both the outcome and the commercial. "I'll be sure to check it out."

He chuckled. "Don't laugh at your old man. TV makes me look like a fool."

"I doubt that," I said honestly. Although I had seen his behind-the-scenes insecure side, my father was a master at public appearances.

"So, what are your plans for today?"

I looked out the window. The weather looked nice, so perhaps we could head to town to do some more research on the box. Then my eyes widened as I did a mental review of today's date. "Abby's birthday is tomorrow! With finals and then the fundraiser, I totally lost track of time."

"I'm sure you'll manage to put together something great. I'll have a present overnighted to her immediately."

To give my father credit, he was the most generous person I knew. It was more than just being able to be so giving, which he obviously was, but he truly enjoyed helping the poor, supporting charities, or making sure that his niece had everything she could possibly want on her seventeenth birthday.

He paused while I, unsure of where the conversation was going, absentmindedly twisted a loose thread in the comforter. "Meredith, I know it might seem like I took on this campaign without consulting with you . . . I knew you were trying to keep your distance when you signed up for summer school, and I especially don't want you to think that you staying there for the summer was my idea."

I held the phone closer to my ear, waiting for him to say more. "Dad, I'm really happy for you. And I know I could have tagged along with you . . . I'll do just that once grandmother decides Abby's proper enough to go home." Just as hard as it was for my father to show sentiment, I suddenly realized it had become equally as hard for me to as well.

"Sounds like a plan. You girls have fun and let me know if you need anything at all, okay?"

"Thanks. You be safe out there."

We hung up and, for a few long minutes, I simply sat on my bed, trying to swallow the lump that had formed in my throat. I tried desperately to bring myself to believe his words, but feeling abandoned was so much easier.

MY PLANS TODAY were clear: find a birthday gift for Abby. How I was going to slip away long enough to do that, however, was a different story. After showering and getting dressed for the day—today I sported navy blue skinny pants with a white and red striped shirt and nautical anchor print scarf—I moseyed down the hall to find her. The door to her room was open, but she wasn't inside. Instead, I saw Tillie changing her linens.

Of all the guest rooms, Abby's was probably the most lavish. A fine crystal chandelier hung over her four-tiered cherry wood bed. Solid wooden furniture made up the rest of the space with gaudy wallpaper lining the walls.

I knocked lightly on the door. "Good morning, Tillie."

She looked up. "Hello, Miss Worthington. How are you today?"

"I'm well, thank you. Have you seen Abby?"

"She just went down to the pool. She didn't want to wake you."

Yes! Abby could easily spend hours at the pool. "I pray she doesn't get sunburned again, who knows what remedy she'll find this time," I said with a smile.

"The milk remedy worked a miracle last time, if I do say so. It was quite unfortunate for the sheets though . . . " She wrinkled her nose, and I chuckled.

"Thanks, Tillie," I said before making my way back to my room.

Abby still thought I was sleeping, which could work to my advantage. Still, I knew there was always a chance she would come looking for me. I would need help distracting her, and who better than her archenemy:

Arthur. I flipped through the contacts on my cell phone and fired off a text to his number.

*Need your help. Tomorrow's Abby's birthday, and I need to go shopping.*

Praying he wasn't busy, I took a seat by the window and spent the next few minutes playing a game of Solitaire, until his reply popped up.

*Tell Agnes you saw her slurping her drink, and you won't see her for a month.*

*After the hell she put us though this week, never. Come on, help me!* As if I was going to rat her out to my grandmother just so she would be whisked away for what would surely be a training in etiquette unlike any other.

A few seconds later, I got my saving grace.

*Fine, I'm on my way. You owe me.*

Smiling, I replied. *You're the best, thank you!*

Then I remembered something, and sent another text. *Hey, did you go back to Herkimer by any chance?*

I had struggled to go back to sleep that night, rubbing my eyes countless times and double-checking, sure I was hallucinating. But no. It was true. There were lights on in the mansion. But how could that be? We hadn't turned on any lights. Heck, we were doubtful the place even had electricity. I was sure Arthur or Jack must have gone back . . .

*No, why?*

*You were in such a hurry that I forgot the diary outside on the table. I thought maybe you went back to get it for me ;)*

*Not me.*

Then it must have been Jack. I grabbed my purse off the closet doorknob, threw my cell phone inside, and scurried down the hall.

Before descending the steps, I peered over the banister at the foyer down below. All clear. Now, if I could just make it down the stairs and out the first door I could find, I would be fine. I bounded down the stairs two at a time and lightly tiptoed across the foyer and out the front door.

"Thank goodness," I muttered. Outside, Bill was leaning up against the same Mercedes that had brought me here from the airport.

"Hi, Bill," I greeted.

He looked up and quickly reached for the door to open it.

"It's okay," I said, "I think I'll drive myself today." I looked around to the side of the estate where the parking lot and garage were located. "Can I use one of the cars?"

"Absolutely," he said. "The keys are in the key cabinet by the garage . . . take your pick."

I thanked him and went on my way. The family owned so many cars and there were so many rings of keys that they needed their own valet-like organizer. Since they all looked practically the same, I grabbed the first set I touched. Then I went to the parking lot in search of my rental, the only thing to guide me being the beep produced by the small panel.

The sound guided me to a blue Jeep—the only Jeep in the lot—when I was startled.

"Planning on stealing my car?"

I whirled around. "Jack!"

He was grinning, and I could feel the hot crimson blush creeping up my cheeks. "I—"

"What I'm wondering is why you'd pick a Jeep? You look more like a Ferrari type of girl," he said, gesturing to the red Ferrari a few cars down.

My eyes widened. I was mortified. "This isn't what it looks like. I wasn't going to steal your car, honest. I asked Bill—"

"I'm only kidding, Meredith."

My cheeks flushed even hotter, and I handed him his keys. He took them and clicked the button to unlock the doors. "I was just heading out to grab a bite to eat. You're welcome to join me."

I realized I hadn't eaten anything yet and was starving. "Thanks, that's really nice of you, but I have to go birthday shopping for Abby. I totally forgot that her birthday is tomorrow and am really crunched for time."

He looked off into the distance, a sheepish look on his face. "I'm actually done here for the day; Carl is finally back. I wouldn't mind driving you, if you wouldn't mind the company."

Although tempted to say yes, my conscience seemed to be guarding my tongue. What would my father think of me gallivanting around town with some guy I barely knew? It wasn't a date, so it's not like I had to worry about that part of it, but still. My father had been very vocal about my involvement with boys, the majority of whom he insisted would always want more from me—especially me. It was a subject we'd long butted heads about, but I now realized this was my chance to prove him wrong.

"Sure," I said. "That would be great."

WE BEGAN OUR outing at Shelley's, a quaint seaside eatery I recalled seeing on Main Street that served fresh fish and lobster. Although allergic to seafood, secretly, I was excited to be trying the local cuisine, to be able to try casual, normal people dining. This restaurant in particular had a cozy feel to it. Around us, the walls were decorated with black and white pictures of fisherman past, of boats and anchors that had sailed these waters. The tabletops were wooden, the legs crafted to look like oars.

"You sure you didn't plan on coming here?" Jack said.

I looked down at my anchor print scarf and chuckled. "Now I feel corny. It was a total coincidence, I swear."

After settling in to our booth, I ordered a strawberry lemonade, and Jack ordered a Coke. We each took a minute to examine the menu, Jack opting for the signature fish fry platter while I went for the chicken fingers.

After we ordered, I set aside my menu. "So, how's your summer shaping up so far? Is the move everything you thought it would be or are you counting the days until you can go back home."

His lips curled into a bemused smile. "It's getting better. I thought for sure I'd bail the first couple weeks. But now I can confidently say that I'm starting to like it."

I took a sip of my drink. "That's good. What about your family? Are they begging you to come home or happy to be rid of you?"

He laughed. "Well, given that it was my dad's hare-brained idea that I go to Harvard, I would hope they don't want me back. My sister's still in Cartwright, so I'm sure she's keeping them company."

"I'm pretty sure I know the answer, but why Harvard?"

Jack leaned back in his seat. "He didn't want me to be stuck in Cartwright all my life given all there is to see outside of it . . . said if I didn't get out now then I'd never work up the courage to leave. If you ask me, I'd say he's living out an unfulfilled dream through me, but it's all good. I definitely can't complain."

I swirled the specs of strawberry around in my glass. "What's your major?"

"So far, architecture with a minor in history, but let's see how the first year goes."

"I'm sure it'll go great. Your father must be proud."

For some reason, his face turned somber. "Thanks, but you're only saying that because you didn't know me in my rebellious phase. I guess I figure I owe my old man since I gave him a pretty hard time."

"It's probably water under the bridge by now. I think parents secretly expect us to act up."

He raised an eyebrow. "Does your father expect you to act up? I doubt he'd be too fond of you sitting here with me." He let his voice trail, his face looking uncharacteristically serious.

"He wouldn't mind," I said lightheartedly, pretending as though I hadn't already wondered the same. "Not that he really sees what I do half the time. It's one of the perks of going to boarding school."

"Boarding school . . . what's that like?"

"I've been going to Phillips Exeter since middle school so honestly, I'm not sure I remember what a regular school is like to be able to tell the difference." I took a sip of my drink. "I'm one of those weird people who enjoys school and there are so many extra curricular activities that in that respect, it's awesome. But despite what the staff says about all students being treated equally, there is a strong sense of entitlement that creates a big divide. Being a Worthington meant that I was automatically accepted on the student council. I get invited to all the exclusive events which, really, I could live without."

Jack seemed intrigued. "Boarding schools are always shown as being so rigid in movies, is it as bad as they make it seem?"

I thought of all the things that went unnoticed in the residence halls and shook my head. "No, we have all the same problems I'd imagine regular schools have. The only difference is that the staff has to think twice on what they want to report to the parents. If it's something really bad, they end up getting the blame for not being in control. If it's minor, it's usually something the parents deny their child was involved in or, if evidence is produced, pay to have covered up. Phillips Exeter has been an unofficial feeder into Harvard for decades so having anything less than a pristine record is frowned upon."

"Is that where you plan to go?"

"I'm not sure if I have a choice to go anywhere else . . . On the one hand, it would be nice to be back in Massachusetts if I go to Harvard. It might even mean I could stay at my father's home in Wellesley but we'll see. As lonely as Phillips Exeter sometimes feels, at least I have a handful of close friends on campus I enjoy hanging out with. Living at home with my father gone as much as he is would only make the reality of my life all the more palpable. No mother, absent father, only child, brutally strict grandparents . . . I try not to give myself a chance to dwell on it but I'd be lying if I said that I don't."

Jack's brown eyes softened and he placed his hand in the middle of the table. "If you do go to Harvard, you can always give me a call if you feel lonely."

"I appreciate it," I said. The conversation had turned heavy, so to change the subject, I asked another question that was bugging me. "Hey, did you happen to go back to Herkimer last night?"

He frowned. "No, why?"

My heart skipped a beat. "I forgot that diary outside."

"Just let me know when, and I'd be happy to take you back to get it."

"You mean that?"

"Sure, the only problem is that I don't really own a boat. I did find a rowboat on the property but it's quite a downgrade if you're used to Arthur's."

Indulging him, I replied, "Hey, a rowboat is good exercise, because clearly you need to work on that."

He laughed. "I know I'm slacking, but you would be too if you had just moved and had no friends. What can I say? I eat my feelings away. Way to make me feel bad."

The waitress approached holding two plates. "A fish fry and chicken tenders?"

I was tempted to laugh considering the irony of her timing. When my eyes met Jack's, a suppressed chuckle escaped my lips.

"That's us," Jack said, eyeing his plate as he rubbed a hand across his incredibly flat stomach. The waitress set the plates in front of us, the smell of battered and deep-fried goodness wafting up.

We each thanked her.

"I'll be back with your drink refills." She picked up our cups and was off.

"This looks so good," I said to Jack, using my bare hands to dig in. Funny how doing so made me feel rebellious.

He took a bite of a fry and nodded his head. "Excellent choice."

We continued eating, engaging in the occasional conversation but mostly savoring the delicious food. When we finished, he paid the waitress, and we left, deciding on a stroll down the bustling string of shops on Main.

On each side of the road, throngs of shoppers—mostly tourists—carried shopping bags or walked small dogs, soaking up the sun and basking in the quaintness that was the Harbor Shops on Main Street.

"Thanks for lunch," I said, looking up at him.

"Thanks for the company," he replied, smiling. "I didn't think I'd make any friends until I started school."

"And I wasn't planning on spending my summer here, trust me. I guess life has a funny way of shaping up."

When we approached the café with an adjacent antique shop, I paused to look in the window. This was the same place the protestors stood the day I'd arrived. Was someone from the protest—I'd have bet anything it was the creepy old man—responsible for the recording that played the night of the gala? Looking at the area now, it looked like any other street corner on Main.

"Do you mind if we stop in there? I'm on a bit of a history kick after seeing Herkimer."

"You know you just want dessert. If I know one thing, it's that girls never say no to chocolate."

I smiled and pulled open the door. "You, my friend, will make someone a happy lady someday."

Beyond the café was shelf after shelf of artifacts: cash registers and butter churns and irons, all waiting for a second chance to find a home. Every time I saw something of interest, I stopped to read the description card that accompanied it. There were clothes and books, hats and china. "I still can't get over how cool the inside of Herkimer was," I said after stopping to admire an old magnifying glass. "And I'm seriously kicking myself for forgetting that diary."

"Just blame the ghosts that freaked Arthur out," Jack said with a knowing smile.

In the distance, I spied a glass case accentuated by display lights. I walked towards it and was suddenly captivated by the glittering jewels behind the glass; they looked every bit as gorgeous as the ones Abby and I had uncovered in the box. I carefully looked at each and every piece, wondering who its former owner might have been, where it had been worn. I was just about to move on when I spied a piece that looked oddly familiar. I frowned and looked at Jack.

"What's up?" he asked.

"This piece over here," I gestured to a lonesome amethyst and diamond earring that was sitting in the case. It could have very well been a brooch, but from the looks of it, it was too small. "It looks like it belongs to one of the sets from that box. The more I look at it, the more sure I am."

Jack shrugged.

"Excuse me," I said to the lady standing behind the other counter. "Can I look at this piece please?" She came over and pulled the elastic key ring from her wrist, unlocking the back lock and sliding the door open.

"Which piece would you like to see?"

I pointed. "That one, please."

"Sure." She took it out and placed it on the glass surface.

I picked it up. "So, this is an earring, not a brooch?"

"It's an earring all right," she confirmed. "Circa 1880. I wish I could say I had the other one, but it was sold to us that way. Still, it's very valuable given the diamond center and ring of amethysts. I suppose it could be made into a brooch, or the jewels could be reset into a ring."

Looking at it now, I was positive that it matched what was in the box. "And how much is it?"

"Five thousand dollars."

The price tag made me flinch. But something deep down in my core told me to buy it; for reasons I couldn't explain, I was sure there was something more to this finding than just mere coincidence. I gulped. "I'll take it."

She proceeded to box it up, looking pleased with her sale, and I wondered how it was that a teenager buying a $5,000 earring was normal to her.

I looked at Jack. "Please don't judge me. I promise I don't normally spend this kind of money. I have no idea what I'm going to do with all those jewels once I finish my research, but for some reason I feel like this earring needs to find its rightful home."

He put a friendly arm around my shoulders and gave me a reassuring squeeze. "I would never judge you."

A SHORT WHILE later, after visiting a few more shops, I settled on a small sentimental present, dissatisfied with what I'd seen in the windows. Shopping for someone who had it all was nearly impossible, so I decided I would surprise her with a trip to the new indoor waterpark in Mashpee. I figured I owed it to her since she hated the ocean and was so easily sunburned when she swam outside.

Jack and I approached his car, and as he reached to open the door for me, something in the reflection of the glass made me freeze. I spun around to look at the tattered gray car that was parked on the opposite side of the road. Inside sat an old man, a man who looked a lot like the one I'd sworn I saw on the property and here on this very street the day I'd arrived. Upon my looking at him, the man receded into the shadow of his seat. I swallowed the lump that had formed in my throat. It had to be the same person. What did he want?

"Whoa!" Jack said suddenly, and I jumped in my spot. "Your nose is bleeding. You okay?" It only took him a few seconds to open the car door, rifle around in the glove compartment, and produce a tissue, which he held to my nose.

"I—I'm all right." Tempted as I was to march right over to the old man and demand to know what he was up to, I knew that wouldn't be smart. He could be armed and dangerous or, worse, working with someone not too far away. Plus, I didn't want to worry Jack.

My hand brushed his as I reached to hold my nose, pulling the tissue away to assess the bleeding. A large crimson stain contrasted the crisp white tissue. A warm trickle rolled through my fingers and down my upper lip.

"Hold your head back," Jack suggested, gently placing a hand behind my head and easing me back.

He stood behind me and let my head rest on his chest, a logical position to relieve the tension from my neck, but one that was also strangely intimate.

Eventually, the bleeding ceased, and I got a mild head rush from lifting my head so quickly.

The car was gone.

"I don't know what happened," I said with a nervous laugh, trying to shake off my anxiety. I desperately wanted to erase that man from my thoughts. But he was ingrained in my mind, and for some odd reason, I couldn't shake the feeling of having seen him before. Long before I ever even arrived in Hyannis Port.

## CHAPTER 6

"Where the hell were you?" Abby demanded when I strode into her room later that afternoon.

"Can't tell," I said with a sly smile. Her birthday present was now tucked away in my bedroom.

"Arthur's been harassing me all morning, and when I went to find you—" She stopped midsentence. "Wait a minute, you put him up to that, didn't you?"

"No comment." But I knew my cheeky grin gave it away.

Her eyes widened. "I cannot believe you! You have some nerve showing your face after pulling that little stunt."

"Well, if you must know, it was for good reason. I actually came to ask for your help," I said, setting the small jewelry box on her desk.

I eagerly watched as she opened the box. At first, her expression registered no recognition. But I had already matched the earring to the pieces and confirmed my hunch.

"I don't get it," she said finally.

"This earring matches one of the ones in the box Jack found. I found it in that antique shop on Main."

"Interesting," she said as she turned it over and examined it. "It's so pretty."

"I know. I wanted your help in sorting out the pieces. I want to take these back there to see if they can tell us more about what seems like an old fashioned safety deposit box."

"I can see Herkimer has really rubbed off on you." She stood up. "Where do we start?"

Half an hour later, we were still sitting around the desk in my room, the jewelry strategically grouped around us. Since starting, we'd sorted every piece and discovered that while some were clearly matching sets, other pieces stood alone. We wrote a brief description of each on a sheet of paper before repacking them back into the box.

"I guess we know what we're doing tomorrow," Abby said once we were done.

I smiled. "I actually have something else in mind for tomorrow."

*THE SUN WAS just beginning to wane overhead, the long day coming to an end. I sat down at the edge of the dock and gazed out at the orange glow in the horizon. I turned to identify the clacking footsteps behind my shoulder and smiled at Abby as she approached.*

*"Meredith, I've been looking everywhere for you," came her cheerful voice.*

*I stood up and walked toward her, my steps becoming a fast jog. As I ran, the sunlight continued to ebb. The faster I ran, the faster the darkness surrounded me, until finally I was no longer running toward Abby but through a forest, a dense loop of what seemed like endless trees.*

*I stopped abruptly, my body jolting forward. Nervously, I looked ahead, but all I could see was darkness.*

*"Hello," I called out shakily. "Hello?"*

*But I heard nothing. It was as quiet as falling snow.*

*Slowly, I turned around, my eyes spanning the expanse for any indication of a path leading outward. In the distance, I saw a flash. I blinked. Was it an illusion? To my relief, when I opened my eyes, I saw the warm glow beckoning me and ran straight toward it.*

*The light grew closer, and soon I was in a clearing just outside of the woodland.*

*I continued to run, propelled by the radiance of the flare. As I approached, I realized that it was not one light that I had seen but several—a cluster of tiny candles lit atop the dense fog-covered ground. Around the candles was darkness, except for the soft aura they cast on the fog, which descended upon the grass like a thick blanket.*

*I kneeled beside the little glass jars, blowing them out for fear of them starting a fire. Just as I was about to put out the last flame, I caught sight of something out of the corner of my eye. A large stone lying flat on the ground. I picked up one of the candles and held it out to see.*

*My eyes widened in horror as I realized that the stone was not there by accident. Before me was a rotted piece of limestone peppered with aged black moss.*

*A grave.*

*I leapt up in fear, my arm giving way, sending my body flying forward. Both arms landed on the ground. As I pulled myself to a standing position, I retrieved the fallen candle, which now cast a glow on several gravestones that surrounded me in every direction. I looked down at my feet and screamed.*

*Beneath my shoes was a mound of fresh dirt—the dirt that I had just landed in. I jumped back off the unmarked grave and stared. Tracked through the soil were imprints from my sneakers and two distinct handprints.*

*Instinctively, I set the candle down and returned to a kneeling position. I began to wipe away my tracks, piling the dirt back and reshaping the mound. Repulsed, I shivered, a wave of nausea flooding me as I realized how fresh the grave looked. It could have been just hours ago . . .*

*I stood up again and reexamined the grave, satisfied that it looked untarnished. Then I walked away, never wanting to look back.*

*"Meredith!"*

*I heard Abby's voice again. This time, I looked up and saw her standing about twenty yards in front of me beside the door to a large mausoleum. Atop the massive marble building was an open armed angel holding a book—the Angel of Death, I presumed. But she was smiling, and despite our surroundings, I felt a wave of relief.*

*I took off in a run toward Abby, forgetting to dodge the headstones that were littered on the ground. Before I knew it, I tripped, and my stomach dropped as I hit the floor with a hard thud.*

*I groaned, my entire body aching. Desperate, I looked around for Abby but was met with the sight of a solid dirt wall. I reached out to touch it, flakes of earth crumbling beneath my fingers.*

*An ear-piercing scream escaped my lips. I pounded on the walls of the tight space, willing them to fall away so I could escape. My gaze turned to the sky, to the faint glow of the moon. I leapt to my feet in the cramped space and raised my hands to see how high I could reach but to no avail.*

*I was six feet under.*

*"Help!" I cried. "Abby! Help! Help!"*

*I frantically kicked and screamed, sheer panic setting in. Horrifying thoughts filled my mind, but I couldn't will them away.*

*Where was Abby? I kept shouting her name, but she never came. My throat burned, but I could not let up.*

*"Help me!" I cried out in desperation.*

*"Shhhh," came a raspy voice.*

*I looked up and in the glow of the moonlight I saw a frail white hand extended down toward me. I could not see the person offering me safety, but without thinking twice, I grabbed their hand, their clench tightening as I struggled to climb up the side of the grave.*

*When I neared the top, another hand reached down to help me, and, both hands securely in the grasp of my savior, I heaved my way out of the grave and onto firm ground. I rolled onto my back, a bubble forming at my throat as I let out a cry of relief.*

*A voice above me spoke. "You will fall into a deep, dark hole."*

*My eyes fluttered open, and kneeling over me was a wispy old woman wearing a dark dress. She had a hunched back and eyes that bore into mine like lasers. Her bony index finger was pointing at me.*

*"Who are you?" My voice was barely a whisper.*

*She didn't so much as blink. "I patrol these grounds, young one. And if you are not careful, you will fall."*

*I pulled myself to a sitting position and fought to find the strength to stand. She did not offer her hand this time; instead, she turned and pointed, and my eyes followed the direction of her long shaky finger.*

*In the distance, a figure was huddled on the ground.*

*"You will fall," she whispered again.*

*Seeing Abby gave me the last push of energy I needed to stand. I carefully hobbled toward her, making extra sure to watch my footing. I was going to make it to her this time—I had to.*

*And I did. When I reached Abby, her back was toward me, and I realized that she was crouched over a grave.*

*"Abby?"*

*She turned around slowly, and that's when I saw it. Over her shoulder the engraving on the headstone read*
WORTHINGTON.

*I gasped. No!*

*That's when I saw Abby's face clearly. Her eyes were swollen and reduced to the size of small slits. On her light shirt I saw round stains where her tears had fallen; it was drenched. A fetid smell filled my nostrils. The smell of fresh earth, of rotting corpses.*

*She said nothing to me. Instead, we stared at each other, my own eyes stinging at the sight of my father's grave. I knelt down to her level and put my hand on her shoulder. It was warm and moist. And sticky. I swiftly released my hand and looked at my palm.*

*Crimson fluid stained my fingertips all the way down to my wrist. I touched my fingers together to feel the texture of the liquid and then smelled it. It was indeed blood.*

*I looked back at her. Blood rapidly flowed from her eyes and fell into her lap, which I only now noticed was fully drenched to the point that a puddle grew on the ground around us.*

*She looked down at herself then back at me, her eyes silently pleading with mine.*

*Someone had done this to her, I was sure of it. I rose to my feet and angrily marched back to where I had fallen.*

*"What did you do?" I screamed viciously to the elderly lady. But she was gone.*

\* \* \*

"HAPPY BIRTHDAY, ABBY," I whispered. It was the morning of Saturday, June fourth, Abigail's seventeenth birthday.

She looked at me sleepily. "What happened to your voice?"

"What do you—" I replied hoarsely. "Oh," I said once I realized that my voice was indeed gruff. "I'm not sure. Laryngitis, I guess."

"You sound pitiful."

"Thanks." I began to laugh, but even that sounded painful. It really wasn't, and I wondered how on earth I had lost my voice this badly.

I'd slept in my own room until abruptly waking up in a cold sweat after what I vaguely recalled was a disturbing dream. Brushing away the odd sense of fear, I'd risen to take a shower. Afterwards, I decided to wake Abby, and here I sat in her room, the sun shining brightly outside of her window.

"Poor you," she said.

"Better me than the birthday girl." I punched her playfully.

"Ow," she whined. "So are you going to tell me where you are taking me?"

I cocked my head to the side and pretended to think. "No," I said simply.

She rolled her eyes, then sat up and looked at my ear curiously. "Hey, your earring is missing."

I raised my hands to feel my ears and noticed that my left one came up empty. "It probably fell off in the shower." I prayed it wasn't really lost. Those heart earrings were one of the few gifts my father had picked out himself. God knows I had received enough stuff picked out by his former secretary, and that woman couldn't shop to save her life. What fourteen-year-old would really want a carpet bag?

Abigail flopped back on her bed and groaned. "Ugh, I'm so tired. I don't want to get out of bed. Can I lie here all day?"

"Nope." I rose and pulled her comforter off her bed, taking it with me as I walked. Underneath she lie curled up in her trademark penguin pajamas. "C'mon, we have a full day ahead of us. Let's get a move on."

FREE FROM THE threat of fish, wildlife, and the blazing sun, I knew Abby would have a ball at Rapids Waterpark, just so long as our grandmother didn't get word of where we were.

After managing to sneak out of the house, we spent the day racing, being catapulted back down the water runs and faux surfing in the giant wave pool. We stopped for the occasional break and to refuel at the snack bar but wasted no time rushing back to the next ride. By the time we reached the parking lot, we were spent.

"I can't move my legs," Abby said as we stiffly forced ourselves into the car. "You know, at this point, I honestly don't even care if grandmother finds out where we went."

Thankfully, Abby had a blast, her praise of the waterpark spewing out of her every time she opened her mouth.

"Don't worry about it. I'll tell her the truth if I have to and hope for the best. I'm more than willing to take responsibility for corrupting her other granddaughter."

A small smile formed on her lips at my comment. "Please," she said nonchalantly. "You don't corrupt me. As far as she's concerned, that ship sailed a long time ago."

I laughed and started the engine. "Don't think I forgot about your present. It's at home waiting for you."

"You didn't have to get me anything!" But her eyes lit up nonetheless.

I took the scenic route back to Greyhurst as I tried my best not to fall asleep at the wheel. According to the clock, we had spent nearly eight hours at the theme park. The sun was beginning to set, the waning orange sphere making its descent right in front of our eyes as I drove down Route 28. Instinctively, I pressed the gas pedal a little harder to get us home before dark.

We were nearly midway through our journey back when I saw it: the familiar gray car in the rearview mirror.

I grabbed Abby's arm. "Don't turn around, but we are being followed." Then I told her about being watched by the man while I was out with Jack.

The man drove slowly, keeping a safe distance but always staying within eyesight. Sure enough, his car followed our every move down the freeway, even taking the same exit, but eventually disappeared as we approached the quiet side roads that led to Greyhurst.

"Should we call the cops?"

"Not this time. The second we do, our freedom this summer is over. But if he shows his face one more time, he's done for," I said resolutely.

HALF AN HOUR later, we were back at Greyhurst. We had every intention of scurrying upstairs unnoticed, but of course, such good fortune did not befall us.

"Welcome back, girls," grandmother said sourly the moment we walked into the house through the tearoom. Of all the places she could have been, she just had to be sitting there. What luck.

It was nearly impossible to read her face: was it surprise, horror, confusion, or just plain displeasure written across her raised eyebrows? "Abigail, darling, did you enjoy yourself today?" She shot a stern glance at me.

There was no way I was going to let Abby get reamed for what was supposed to be her day.

"I took her to Rapids." I dreaded looking my grandmother in the eye but knew I had to stand on firm ground.

"Rapids?" It took her a few seconds before a look of clarity washed over her face. "Why on earth would you girls go to *Rapids*?"

Abigail started to open her mouth, but I immediately cut her off. "To celebrate Abby's birthday. I wanted to treat her to something fun."

"Gallivanting around with hoodlums in that germ-infested water is *fun*? And to think you went and lost your voice. Oh dear, whatever will your father say." With that, she rose. "I expect that you'll want to wash up. Perhaps then you could join us for a *proper* birthday celebration."

We turned on our heels like the obedient granddaughters we were expected to be and proceeded—or rather crawled—upstairs.

"That went better than I thought," I said dully, feeling exhausted and deflated.

Upon showering off all the grime of the pool water, we dressed in our dinner formal wear and made our way down the winding steps and through the lavish living room to meet our waiting grandparents.

Grandmother sat in her usual spot at the head of the table, grandfather in his wheelchair beside her. In the center of the large table was an exquisite two-layer jewel tone cake with flowers adorning the top tier. The words "Happy Birthday, Abigail" were elegantly scrolled across the side of the cake in glittery white icing. Stacks of wrapped presents also sat on the table; my present, on the other hand, I kept tucked upstairs, preferring not to have my grandparents' judgmental watch.

After dinner, the cake was cut without the traditional singing of *Happy Birthday*, per our grandmother's instructions. We ate the luxurious vanilla chiffon cake and then a beaming Abigail unwrapped her presents. She received clothes, jewelry, books, trinkets, a purse, and various electronics, most from her parents but some sent by our uncles and then, of course, our grandparents. The last gift on the table was tiny, and as she lifted it, I spied my father's unique version of the Worthington family seal.

"Oh my," Abby gasped when she saw what it contained. Inside the box sat a bottle of one of the most expensive perfumes in the world: the pyramid shaped Baccarat Les Larmes Sacrees de Thebes. The one-ounce bottle cost nearly six grand.

"Wow. That's—" Abby paused and swallowed. "So nice of uncle Magnus."

Later that night, when we were back in my room, I pulled out her present and handed it to her.

She delicately unwrapped the gold paper, revealing a brown cardboard box. Inside was a porcelain oval jewelry box with "Happy Birthday" hand painted in the center of a plethora of raised glittering flowers and butterflies. Inside that sat the other part of my present: two tiny porcelain figurines holding hands. Underneath they were attached to the word "Sisters."

"Oh!" Abby gasped. "It's beautiful! I love it."

I raised my glass of hot chocolate that we had snuck up from the kitchen. "Here's to the next year."

"To the next year," Abby repeated as our mugs clinked.

But had I known what would be in store for me just a week from now, I would not have been so cheerful.

CHAPTER 7

"Meredith, dear, have you decided where you'll be studying after you finish at Phillips Exeter?" my grandmother's friend, Alice, asked. We were seated outside where the staff had set up an elaborate brunch assortment that included champagne and sorbet floats, orange-cranberry scones, smoked salmon and herb cheese sandwiches, heirloom tomato tarts, brioche French toast with fresh figs, and a charcuterie board. It had been nearly an hour since the last plate was cleared and yet here we sat, our teacups sitting untouched on the white linen tablecloth, as my grandmother's guests engaged in mindless discussion that revolved around the same three topics: money, status, and gossip.

Alice turned towards the two other ladies seated to her right. "Marianne's daughter, Lauren, was all set to go to Harvard until the news broke that Yale had become the top law school in the country. Can you believe it took *two* phone calls to get everything lined up at the last minute? Clearly things aren't as easy as they used to be in our day."

With that, all three ladies turned towards me and I had three expectant stares. "Well, Meredith, it seems you now have a problem on your hands. You've got a difficult decision to make," Arthur's mother said.

Choosing between following in my father's footsteps or attending the nation's top school was hardly my idea of having a problem, but I remained polite. "I haven't given it much thought," I said casually. "Besides, the bigger decision to me is whether I want to go to medical school or pursue a degree in English."

It was entertaining watching their eyes dart nervously to my grandmother, who sat at the head of the table. She dismissed my statement with a light flick of her hand. "It's obvious Meredith has not yet realized the importance of tradition. I expect that by summer's end she will have an entirely different outlook." Her jaw hardened as she fixed the napkin so it was evenly resting in her lap.

"You must be careful of who you let fill your head with nonsense, Meredith. Outsiders can't be counted on to understand our values and traditions. You are keen to keep your circle of acquaintances contained to Abigail and Arthur this summer." Arthur's mother took a sip of her tea. "Of course, Alice's daughter would be a fine influence as well. Just don't lower yourself to my son's level by associating yourself with our *gardener*. Why, I nearly fired the boy on the spot when Arthur said he'd spent the afternoon with him the other day. My son might be successful, but he's been impulsive since the day he was born."

Alice and Bethany laughed. "A gardener!" Bethany exclaimed. She had no children herself, per her own accord. "Oh my word."

Abby, who was seated on my left and who had remained near silent the entire brunch, kicked my leg under the table. "They're horrible," she whispered.

"He's lucky you *didn't* fire him," Alice added.

"If I did then Agnes and I both would be understaffed. We can't have our shrubs looking overgrown," Arthur's mother said.

"Now Belinda, you know good help isn't hard to find . . . for the right price," my grandmother responded. Then she stood, a clear indication she was done with the subject. "Have I shown you my newest Monet?"

The three ladies stood and trailed behind my grandmother like baby ducks following their parent. Abby and I begrudgingly got up as well and rounded out the line. To an outsider, I was almost positive we looked like a scene out of *Make Way for Ducklings* as we made our way across the covered patio, through the massive doors leading inside to the music room where we proceeded to sit for yet another hour over yet another pot of tea.

Respite finally came when my grandmother left to ask the staff to box up some of the chocolate she had just had flown in from Switzerland for her guests to take home, a cue that it was time for them to leave.

"Do excuse us as we go practice our piano lessons," I said as I stood. Abby was not far behind.

"It's been lovely spending the afternoon with you," Alice said.

"The pleasure has been ours," I lied. By now I was flawless at sounding polite.

After a nod and a smile at each of the ladies, Abby and I slowly walked to the door. It wasn't until we rounded the corner and were out of view that we both looked at each other and exhaled in relief. Just as I was about to walk away, I heard Bethany speak.

"That one is just as wild as her mother. *Medical school?* What a disgrace that would be. It's a good thing Magnus drove Lillian off before she had time to sink her common ways into Meredith," she said.

"I couldn't help but wonder if that recording that aired was referencing how he took care of her. Maybe he locked *Lillian* up somewhere," Arthur's mom said.

"He certainly has the money and status to make it happen," Alice added.

My eyes widened and I looked at Abby. Just like that, they had covered it all: money, status, and gossip. Except this time their words made me physically sick to my stomach.

AFTER GRANDMOTHER'S SLEEK black limousine pulled out of the wrought iron gates, Abigail turned to me eagerly. "Free at last!"

Once again we'd spent our week subjected to our grandmother's agenda. Only this time she had seen to it that Abby and I paid the price—and then some—for our waterpark excursion.

Now we were finally free. For tonight at least. This morning at breakfast our grandmother had announced that she would be headed to Boston to assist my father with the conventions, and that they both would be back tomorrow night. She also announced that a few weeks from now there would be another gala celebrating the Fourth of July.

"The staff will get you fitted for your dresses," she'd said as she stood from the breakfast table. "It seems you both have put on a bit of weight since the last gala." She had made no attempt to hide her disdainful look.

At the memory, I grabbed Abigail's hand and gave it a squeeze. "I don't know about you, but I want to get as far away from this house as I can. If I have to see another teacup and scone I think I'm going to lose it."

During our sequester, Jack had been my only release. Abby and I secretly met him a couple times in the garden, where he entertained us with humorous tales of his rambunctious childhood in Canada, relaying everything from the time he accidentally drank lighter fluid at age four to the time he added pebbles to his mother's stew when she wasn't looking. "I was forever banished from the kitchen after that," he'd said. Those brief escapes, along with phone calls with Jack, had kept me sane. What started off as two-minute calls to coordinate on when we'd meet outside got progressively longer as the days went by, and I couldn't help but think about him when we weren't speaking.

Abby pulled out the bobby pins that strategically held her hair in an elegant chignon at the nape of her neck, then moaned as she massaged her scalp. "Ugh, that is so much better."

Poor Abby, being punished for having unruly hair. My own hair was limply held back with a white headband. God forbid my bangs hung over my eyes. I flung off the blazer I wore over my teal tank top and skinny jeans and swung it over my arm. "Won't be needing that."

We spent our morning shopping, stopping only when our stomachs wouldn't let us go any farther for an indulgent lunch, a far cry from all the healthy crap we'd been forced to eat under our grandmother's watch. Happily filled up on burgers, steak fries, and milkshakes from Scotty's, we sat in the restaurant and debated where to go next.

"I don't know if it's just me being rebellious, but I feel like doing something adventurous," I said.

Abby shrugged. "Like what?"

"No idea, I just dread the idea of going back to Greyhurst already." I glanced at the flat screen television mounted to the wall behind Abby's head. A Monty's Sporting Goods commercial flashed on the screen, and I tuned it out as I went over several possibilities in my head. Then, a picture of a tent appeared on the screen, and I called out, "Camping!"

Abby frowned. "*Camping*?"

"It would be so much fun! Just think, you and I camping somewhere on the property. We could get tents and make s'mores and play games." I was giddy with excitement.

"I hate to burst your bubble, but you do realize that grandmother probably has the staff instructed to watch our every move. We'd get busted for sure and then she'd be back here so fast we wouldn't be allowed out of her sight for a month." The skin around Abby's big green eyes crinkled warily. She must have seen my deflated look, because she added, "Why not spend the night in the guest house?"

The guesthouse, of course! On the property was a small beachfront cottage that was supposed to be for visitors, but was never used. The size of the simple little house was clearly not up to my grandmother's standards, which is why I knew she would never dare subject any of our guests to it. Had it not been tucked far enough away on the property where people couldn't actually see it, she probably would have had it torn down altogether.

"It's sort of like camping if you think about it, only with actual walls. I would feel a lot better with walls."

I chuckled. "Fine."

A TRIP TO the grocery store was in order, so after paying for our food, we hauled our shopping bags back to the car. Abby and I stopped by the local supermarket where we bought all of our favorite foods and some games. Then we came home, packed our things, and made our way outside to our home away from home.

The sun was shining brightly as we eagerly strode across the lawn with our clothes and food supply. When we cleared the trees, we saw the one-roomed beach house on the far end of the property.

The door to the house was unlocked, and we eagerly made our way inside. Although unoccupied, the inside of the small house was well decorated and clean; it even had a hint of a rustic feel to it. There were two queen size beds sitting side by side, separated by a wooden nightstand. A bathroom sat off to the right, just opposite the kitchenette.

"Wow, this is perfect," Abby exclaimed. "Too bad we couldn't live here all summer."

"Yeah, I know. That would be sweet."

The cottage didn't have an air conditioner, and the inside of the house felt balmy from being closed up for so long. We dropped our bags on the bed, unpacked our food, and cracked open the windows, marveling at the beautiful sea view.

I was about to turn away but did a double take as, in the distance, I saw Jack walking along the water, the rope in his hand pulling a boat.

"Jack!" I called from the window, waving my hand in the air. At first he didn't acknowledge me, his face muscles tense. I called his name again, louder this time, and he looked up.

"Over here!" I said, and then rushed outside.

"Look what I found," he called out to me as I approached. "I guess now you can get your diary back without bothering Arthur for a ride."

I squealed with excitement. "Where'd you get that?"

"I stumbled across a dilapidated shed on the west rim of the property." His strong arms almost popped out of his short-sleeved T-shirt as he came to a stop.

"Do you think it works?" I asked.

He shrugged. "It should once it gets gassed up. There are a couple gallons in the utility shed. Not sure if you have any afternoon plans, but I'd be happy to take you back to Herkimer once I get this baby powered up." He smiled, revealing handsome dimples.

I looked to Abby, who had joined us outside. "I'll go if you go."

"I'll drive careful, I promise," Jack added when Abby's face paled.

She looked out at the water, which thankfully appeared relatively calm today. "It's not the water I'm worried about. It's the fish . . . " She paused, chewing on her bottom lip. "I really would like to see Herkimer, though . . . "

"Don't feel forced into going," I said.

"No, no, it's fine," she said confidently. "I want to."

"Quick, Jack, let's go before she changes her mind."

DESPITE JACK'S EVERY attempt to make the ride over to Herkimer as smooth as could be, Abby spent the entire first half of the ride keeled over the side of the boat, retching.

"Should we turn around? She's not doing so great," Jack asked quietly as he cut the engine in the middle of the ocean. Abby's cheek—the only part of her I could see—was clammy and pale. I couldn't imagine subjecting her to the rest of the ride to Herkimer *and* the whole way back.

"Yeah, I think we should. I feel so bad . . . "

Jack powered the engine back up and slowly turned the boat around.

"We're going back," I said to Abby, pulling her hair out of her face. "I'm so sorry, honey."

She sat up, wiping her mouth. "No, I'm sorry; I didn't think I would get sick. I haven't been on a boat in ages. Figures this would happen."

"It's okay, we'll be back to the cottage in no time, and then we can get you in bed."

She frowned, steadying herself against the edge of the boat. "You're not stepping one foot off this boat. I'll be fine once we make it to land. You are going to get that diary."

I couldn't help but scoff. "Whatever. I'm not leaving you after you just spent the last ten minutes puking your guts out."

She shook her head. "In case you forgot, I want to read that diary just as much as you do. And you are going to go get it for me."

"Wow, well, if it's an order—"

"It is," she said firmly, and I knew she wasn't going to let up.

"All right then, I'll get you the diary, Your Majesty. But I'll be back before you know it so don't you overdo it."

Although she looked weak and drained, she smiled.

90

"OKAY, LET'S TRY this again," Jack said after we'd made sure Abby was safely on dry land and resting comfortably in the guest house. "Ready?"

"I'm ready." I held my hair together at the nape of my neck as he revved the boat and we zipped away from the coast. He was a skilled boater, his every move seeming to come with such ease. I smiled contently. The fact that my summer had momentarily turned into this was something to be grateful for. Never in my wildest dreams would I have thought that I would be sitting here now, on a boat in someplace as beautiful as Hyannis Port with someone like Jack.

"Thank you," I thought, not realizing that I'd also said it out loud.

Jack turned back to look at me. "For what?"

My face flushed. "Everything. From the first day I got here, you've been so kind to me. This summer's been a little crazy to say the least."

"I'm really glad you decided to stay."

He said he was happy I'd stayed; he didn't say anything about Abby. My heart skipped a beat, but just as quickly, I warned myself against reading too much into his reply. "Me too."

"I'm also pretty stoked I finally get to enjoy normal summer weather. My sister called yesterday and said it was still snowing in Cartwright."

"In June?" I asked incredulously. I had no idea where Cartwright was but made a mental note to Google it later.

"Yeah, it's not unheard of this time of year. Just depends on how bad of a winter we had."

I shook my head. "I don't think I could live in a place where there isn't at least a few months of warm weather. It sounds too depressing."

"You're not alone. Our population isn't even close to a thousand people and the majority are over fifty. It's not really sustainable for the younger generation. My sister was always planning on leaving until she fell for Peter. They'd been in every class together since they started school but never gave each other the time of day. One day he asked her to the movies and they've been together ever since. They married a little over a year ago, and I think my parents are finally coming around to him and the idea of her sticking around."

"They don't like him?" I asked.

"They do, but they thought he was robbing her of her future. Peter's a great guy but he'll never leave Cartwright. His family's been there just as long as mine have and he's been primed from his youth to take over his family's drilling business. Lucy knew that from the get-go, though, so at the end of the day it was her decision."

"Does she work?"

"She's a teacher. Honestly, I can't imagine her doing anything else. Growing up I can't tell you how many times I was forced to sit in her makeshift classroom as one of her students. Her other students, mind you, were stuffed animals so naturally that put me at the top of my class." He smirked. "I knew my ABCs by the age of two."

"Show off."

"I knew how to read before I even started school."

I laughed. "Okay, now you're just gloating."

"Hey, at least give me that. She used to make me sit through some pretty awful cooking classes where she'd make me wear an apron and everything. Then she'd make me eat some pretty repulsive recipes."

"Like what?" I asked.

"Bread with mayonnaise, cheese, and strawberry jelly. Cereal in orange juice with bacon bits sprinkled on top. The worst part of it was I couldn't even tell my parents about all her torture because she'd threaten to give me an F in her fake gradebook and she said I'd never be admitted to kindergarten. I was gullible enough to believe her."

"That's horrible!"

"We're close now if that's any consolation. She's five years older than me so eventually we both matured and discovered we could be friends."

"I'm glad it all worked out in the end."

He smirked. "For the most part."

Jack parked the boat by the dock just like Arthur had done a few days earlier. "I can run up and grab the book for you, if you'd like. I know you don't want to waste any time getting back to Abby."

"You sure? You've already done so much . . . "

"Where did you say you left it?"

"On the table by the door. The one with the creepy dolls."

"Ah, yes. The dolls . . . " He climbed out of the boat. "I'll be back in a flash."

Only it wasn't a flash. Nearly twenty minutes later, and he still was not back. Could it be that he was still trying to find it? An odd feeling washed over me. Something didn't seem right; I felt it in my gut.

After double-checking to make sure the boat was secured, I carefully walked down the dock and up the small hill. I squinted into the distance, my pulse quickening at the sight.

Jack!

## CHAPTER 8

When I saw Jack's limp body face down on the ground, I screamed. My knees threatened to buckle beneath me, but I mustered all my strength to sprint across the lawn. The distance seemed about a hundred miles long, and with each passing microsecond, my mind raced like a drum roll.

Once I reached his lifeless body, I rolled him onto his side and gasped. Across the back of his head was a deep gash oozing blood. A crimson puddle had formed below him. I cradled his head into my arms. "Jack! Jack! Are you okay?"

He lay motionless, his head heavy against my palms. How could this have happened?

I was dizzy with panic, my ears ringing so loud that it masked the loud pounding of my heart. Hastily, I yanked the headband from around my hair and used it to apply pressure to his head, praying he would open his eyes. "Jack, please answer me . . . what happened?"

His body still lay flaccid on the ground. To be sure, I put my ear to his chest and listened for a heartbeat. A steady, rhythmic beat met my ears and filled me with relief, but it was thudding at a snail's pace. Anxious, I removed the headband tourniquet to assess his wound;

the cloth was soaked, blood still dripping down the side of his head.

I had to get him to a hospital—fast. But we were stuck on this island hundreds of feet away from the dock and miles away from the nearest hospital. My cell phone was still in the guest house, and this house . . . there was obviously no way to call for help. I frantically searched Jack's pockets, only to realize he didn't have a phone on him either.

Without thinking twice, I grabbed Jack under his arms and pulled with all my might, slowly sliding his unresponsive body across the grass. It didn't take much to leave me gasping for breath; obviously someone with my build was attempting the impossible. If only someone like Arthur was here to help.

What seemed like an eternity later, we neared the boathouse, and I collapsed to the ground. I let out a whimper—my arms burned like fire, my legs stung like acid.

Whitecaps formed at the peaks of the tall waves as the wind blew violently around us. High tide must have been blowing in. The boat swayed in the water and it dawned on me that getting back to Greyhurst would be impossible in these conditions. There was also the predicament of how to get Jack down the rickety dock and into the boat.

*Oh God, oh God! What do I do? How can I possibly drag him down this dock and into the boat!*

Tears streamed down my face. What if something happened to him? What if I couldn't get him the help he needed and he didn't recover? I lifted Jack's arms as high as I could to protect his head and walked backwards down the dock, dragging his body.

"Somebody please help me," I cried out weakly to nobody but myself. In my state of panic, I looked out across the water desperately, searching, praying that help would miraculously appear. But there was nothing on the horizon.

I screamed out in frustration. How on earth would I do this? But I had to. I caught sight of his face and my screams of frustration turned into sobs. Jack's masculine features, his structured, chiseled jaw, were covered with crimson blood. All of those things that made him distinctly Jack, distinctly strong, were so feeble now.

I was trembling, panic consuming my every nerve, as I bent over him.

"Jack, please, please." My voice came out as a croak. "I need you to wake up. Please—" I began to sob again, this time uncontrollably, the anguish of the situation becoming more than I could bear. I stroked his bloody forehead, my hands becoming sticky.

Then, with a new wave of determination, I wiped away my tears and stood up. There had to be a way off this blasted island. I broke out into a full run, looking for more level ground where I could lead the boat and get Jack into it. A part of me was thankful I had once been an avid runner; I needed every fraction of every second I could get.

I ran the entire expanse of the island, eventually ending up behind the dilapidated mansion where the view of the ocean stretched out as far as my eyes could see. Not only was the entire island elevated, but there was not one direction in which I looked that indicated land was nearby.

I quickly scanned the ledge again, assessing the height and trying to determine what the lowest point of the island was. Just as I was about to race back to Jack, a red glimmer caught my eye. I looked up and squinted. In the distance, an abstract shape bobbed in the water, appearing to get closer. A few moments later, a boat materialized in front of me. Two flags waved on the boat's stern, one red and one white. The boat sped through the water like a shooting cannon and seemed to be headed toward the island.

"HELP!" I screamed. "HELP!"

I continued to cry out, jumping and flailing my arms in the air. "Please! Help!"

Much to my relief, they were still proceeding my way. What felt like an eternity later but was only really about a minute, the boat careened up to the ledge.

"We received a call for assistance," the blue uniformed man called out. He pulled out his walkie-talkie and mumbled some code words to the receiving end.

"Yes! Please hurry, this way!" I ran at full speed along the edge on the grass as the boat followed me in the water. When he was in view, I pointed at Jack's body on the ground and the boat sped past me. I continued to run as fast as I could, stunned as a group of uniformed men swiftly descended from the Coast Guard boat and swarmed around him, blocking my view. I tried to peer around them to see what was happening but only heard a lot of simultaneous talk. Tears streamed from my eyes and blinded my vision—it was all like a cruel nightmare.

Before I knew what was happening, they had Jack on a gurney and were skillfully lowering him into their boat.

"Ma'am, I need you to follow me," said the last man to descend.

I did as I was told, and with their help, followed their steps.

Paramedics placed Jack on an anchored stretcher inside a covered canopy and began working in sync while the same man stayed behind to talk to me.

"Can you please give me a detailed account of what led to his injury?" He had a clipboard and a stern expression.

"Is he going to be okay?" I blurted out.

The man looked annoyed, but then his expression softened. "I understand your concern. We are still trying to determine what's wrong. I need you to give me his information as well as a detailed account of what happened."

I tried to gather my thoughts but was so scatterbrained that it took exceptional effort. "His name is Jack Saunders. He is eighteen years old."

"Any known health problems?" He quickly jotted notes in his pad.

"No, none that I know of."

"Date of birth?"

"November twelfth."

"Current medications or medication allergies?"

"I don't think so, but I'm not sure." It was at this moment that I wished I had known Jack for longer than I did.

"Is the patient intoxicated or under the influence of any drugs?"

"No, absolutely not."

"Okay," he said, checking off boxes. "Now please recount the last thirty minutes for me."

The last thirty minutes? I didn't even know how much time had elapsed since I found him unconscious. I, myself, didn't know what had happened to him.

"We came out for a boat ride and decided to stop by the island for a quick walk."

"The island is private property, ma'am. Did you go inside the house?"

I bit my lip, thinking of the last time when we'd gone inside. "No, no we did not. We stayed out on the lawn. I went to get something from our boat and when I came back around I saw him sprawled on the floor."

"Did you see anyone else on the island? Or anything that could have fallen and injured him?"

"No, nothing at all," I replied, although in my haste I hadn't really looked.

"And your name is?"

I froze. "My name?" I replied stupidly. In my desperate attempt to save him, I hadn't even realized what this meant—thankfully the technician hadn't recognized me. Would word get out to my father? Should I lie?

He raised a curious eyebrow. "Yes, ma'am. Your name."

"Jill. Jill—" I looked around. "Saunders," I said hastily.

"Jill Saunders?"

"Yes." I needed a name that Jack would recognize, a last name at least.

"Chris?" came a rushed voice.

The man in front of me turned away and my heart raced. Peering behind him, I craned my head to listen to the verdict.

"His vitals are stable," I heard the man whisper. "But we still need to get him to the emergency room A-SAP. We are going to go via the northeastern channel." I hadn't realized I'd been holding my breath until I exhaled in relief. Jack was all right. Wasn't he? I stumbled back to my chair and collapsed in a heavy heap as they began discussing the logistics of their route. Tired, I leaned back in my chair, my head slumping back against the glass. My eyes stared blankly ahead at the water quickly passing me by, but I was too exhausted—on every dimension—to react. I wouldn't rest until he was awake, until he could talk to me and tell me what happened. Until I knew he would recover.

The technician rejoined me soon after and relayed the news I had already heard. "We still are unsure about what happened and need to take him to the ER for diagnostic testing. He is still unconscious, and it's a pretty serious wound he has there. We want to make sure he hasn't suffered any damage as a result of the head trauma."

Damage. Trauma. Those words shook me to my core. "Thank you." I smiled weakly. "Can I see him?" I asked hopefully. His professional demeanor seemed unyielding, so I begged. "Please—"

His expression softened. "Right now, I think it's best that they continue to monitor him until we get to the pier. Once we are there, you can ride with him in the ambulance." He paused, then continued. "Are you absolutely positive that you didn't see anyone on the island, someone who could have done this to him?"

My heart sank. Surely he couldn't be insinuating that I had something to do with this. Suddenly I wanted nothing more than to be near Jack; it felt like a huge hole had been poked through my heart leaving it empty . . . wanting. I longed to see his eyes open, to talk to him like I could before this nightmarish day began. "No, I didn't see anyone."

Chris patted my shoulder and turned to leave.

Then I remembered something. "Hey—"

He looked back at me.

"Did you say that someone phoned you?"

"Yes, ma'am. We received an anonymous call for assistance on the island."

"Anonymous—" I echoed as he walked away.

As I sleepily lay my head against the glass window of the boat, I couldn't get two nagging questions out of my head. Who had called the Coast Guard? Who was onto us?

NOT EVEN FIVE minutes later, we made it on land to a medical loading dock far from Greyhurst where there was a waiting ambulance to take us to the Cape Cod General Hospital. Jack was still unconscious, but as I sat by his side in the speeding ambulance I noticed the color creeping back into his face. His skin was now cleaned, the pearls of caked blood gone from his hairline and brow.

My hand in his, I spoke to him, told him the things that I wanted so badly to believe: that everything would be okay, that his health was now entrusted to trained professionals who would *make* it okay.

During the ride, I couldn't take my eyes off of his stat monitors.

The technician who was tending to him smiled at me reassuringly. "His stats are within normal limits and that is a very good sign."

I took a deep breath and buried my face against Jack's arm. The vehicle must have been zipping down the street, but from inside it was as sturdy as an army tank.

When the ambulance halted, everything happened so fast. The double doors flew open to reveal a slew of waiting hospital staff members who, once his gurney was wheeled onto the ground, whisked Jack away.

A blast of warm, sticky air filled the ambulance, and I watched in horror as he was rolled into the hospital. Was their haste any indication of the seriousness of his condition? Dread sank deeper into my gut. Of course it was. That's what ambulance riders were there for—*emergencies*.

A pretty blonde woman holding a clipboard suddenly appeared in the doorway of the ambulance and escorted me to a waiting room where I was to patiently sit until his tests were over.

The process was taking much longer than I expected, and today I was anything but patient. I paced back and forth in the bright white hallways, my thoughts never straying from Jack. The last couple weeks continuously replayed in my mind like an antique movie reel. From the first time I met him to the crazy things we'd seen and heard about Herkimer and finally, *this* happening. We were on to something—I now felt it with every fiber of my being. I couldn't, for the life of me, though, think of what it could be.

There was something significant to the mansion's history that we needed to figure out. The Coast Guard had mentioned that it was private property, which I knew, but everybody knew that it was *abandoned* private property. How did people not know that it had in fact been lived in, that it was an archaic piece of history left to rot? I shuddered to think we had stumbled upon something big enough that someone would have to resort to such an act to keep us away. And then there was the mystery of who called the Coast Guard. Could Abby have had some sort of premonition that we were in trouble? I still had yet to call her.

The guilt of Jack's condition weighed heavy on my heart as I continued to pace. Around me, people rushed from one end of the hall to the other while I continued to walk slowly, my feet in perfect sync. Stretchers whizzed by. Professionals donning white-coats, which blended in with the pale white walls that surrounded me, sped through the hallways. Nurses floated from room to room carrying food trays, IV poles, crash carts, and charts. In all the commotion, my eyes searched for only one thing: Jack.

What seemed like nearly two hundred laps around the hall later, I heard a familiar name being called in the waiting room.

"Jill Saunders?" came a strong male voice. I turned around only to realize that no one had responded. And that's when the realization hit me. Jill Saunders was me; it was my alias.

"Yes!" I called as I raced back to the room. The man was wearing a white coat, the lapel indicating that his name was Dr. Frank Peters.

"Ms. Saunders, I would like to speak to you regarding Jack Saunders," he said. I tried to read his expression, tried to decipher his every move.

"Is he okay?" I spat out the words.

He gently took my arm and we began to walk, presumably toward Jack's room. "He is stable and has regained consciousness. He has a pretty serious concussion; it's quite some injury he sustained from that beam. We administered ten stitches to his head and want to keep him overnight for observation . . . just until we are sure the concussion is no longer a threat."

Tears pricked my eyes. Concussion. *Threat.* More words I could not bear to hear. "But it's not a serious threat anymore, right?"

"Shouldn't be, but concussions are tricky. We're doing everything we can to monitor his situation."

We stopped at a door with a vertical window. I glanced inside and saw the end of a stretcher, feet tucked into the crisp white sheet.

The doctor spoke to me again. "You may go in. He is still a little groggy but appears to be fully lucid. If for some reason you don't think he sounds right, you let us know immediately. Confusion is often a symptom of a head injury, so we'll want to watch it. So far, so good, though."

"Thank you, doctor," I said as I opened the heavy door and tip-toed inside.

I wasn't prepared for the sight I saw. Jack was propped up on a thick white pillow, small oxygen tubes in his nose. The attending nurse stood by his side, programming the computer monitor to his right. In his muscular arm was an IV connected to a tall pole alongside his bed. His face was pallid, his hair unkempt. A large bandage covered most of his forehead. His eyes were now closed, and I quietly shuffled to his side, careful not to wake him.

As I made my final step, his eyes fluttered open. Our gazes met, and it took all my effort not to throw myself in his arms.

A weak smile formed at his lips.

"Meredith . . . " His deep voice sounded hoarse.

"Oh, Jack . . . " I sat beside him. "I am so sorry."

"It's not your fault," he replied softly. He feebly tried to pull himself up in his bed.

I waited until the nurse excused herself before I spoke more. "I feel like it is all my fault." I looked at him sadly. "I should never have pushed you to take me to the island."

"Your fault?" he whispered. "It's because of you that I'm in safe hands now. How on earth did you get me here?"

I relayed the story to him while he silently listened.

"You are so amazing," he said once I had finished.

I smoothed out his sheet. "Amazing? Oh God, no. I've never felt lower in my life." My shoulders hung in dismay. "I was so scared. I didn't know what to do. How do you feel now?"

"Tired. Sore." He rubbed his head. "I just hope I don't have to stay here long."

"The doctors want to keep you here overnight for precaution's sake. I will stay here with you for as long as I can, and then I'll come visit you first thing in the morning. Besides, you should rest. Don't worry about work or anything, I'll make sure my grandmother knows."

"I'm off tomorrow anyways. Besides, I'm actually looking forward to work. I'm determined to get to the bottom of this."

I frowned. "I'm not sure that I follow. The doctor said—"

"I lied," Jack said. "It wasn't an accident, Meredith. Someone purposely hit me from behind, I just wish I could've seen who."

His words hit me like a ton of bricks. The lights that I'd seen on at night. The culprit. Was it the same person?

"We need to tell the police," I said, an angry fire lighting within me. "The person needs to be caught."

His face turned serious, and he reached out to hold my hand. My heart skipped a beat. "Meredith, telling the police would only get you into trouble, and I'm not willing to do that. If I could say I was there alone,

105

maybe. But they would find out the truth from the paramedics."

"But—" I started.

Jack lowered his voice and said, "I really think someone is trying to protect something—the police will not care about some abandoned old property. Just do me a favor . . . please promise me you won't go back to that house. Ever. This has turned serious, and we cannot pretend that it's safe there. So please, promise me. Whoever it was, and for whatever reason they did this to me, I'll handle it. For all we know, you could have been the target, and I would never forgive myself if I didn't do something about it."

I stiffened. He wasn't going to back down, of that I was sure.

"I promise," I lied.

THAT NIGHT, LONG after Abby had crawled into bed—our plans on staying in the guest house were obviously called off—I lay in bed myself, exhausted and spent, but unable to sleep. Poor Abby had been beside herself at the news of Jack's hospitalization, but had been adamant that she had not called the paramedics. Just another mystery in this already convoluted plot. I sighed and rose from my spot, looking down at the landscape below that was lit by the garden lights, which now cast a white glow in the black night. I scanned the panorama, making out the faint coast of the ocean as my eyes adjusted to the darkness. As I gazed in the direction of Herkimer, a surge of electricity went up my spine. I knew exactly what I had to do.

## CHAPTER 9

I tried to keep my mind from talking me out of my journey as I traipsed through the dark woods toward the water, listening to the sounds of the night. The chirping of the crickets, the rustling of leaves, the croaking of the frogs on the shore—all seemed to beg me to turn around, to go back to the safety of my room. A big part of me felt like I was betraying Jack after I'd promised not to go back. Not to mention Abby, who would flip if she knew where I was going— the pillows I'd strategically placed under my blanket were to fool her just as much as the staff. I knew she would have insisted on coming, but I couldn't do that to her, not after the last time had made her so violently ill.

Going alone wasn't the smartest move, and I knew that; if I met the same fate as Jack, there would be no one to help. Navigating the deep waters would be challenging, but I would have to muster the courage somehow. For Jack's sake and for the sake of whatever odds we were up against.

As I reached the water's edge, I realized that the boat that had taken us to our perilous doom earlier that day was still roped off at the island. I shone the light into the trees, vaguely remembering that Jack mentioned finding a rowboat somewhere on the southwest side of the property and set off on my quest. With my flashlight and a baseball bat in tow, I raced around the west rim of the property through the overgrowth that paralleled alongside the forest. When I finally came across the old dilapidated shed where Jack had said he found the first boat, I raised the light to the overgrown weeds, and there it was: a canoe. Wasting no time, I pulled the heavy rowboat all the way to shore and into the dark ocean then sloshed through the water and hopped aboard.

Once situated, I positioned the flashlight to illuminate the path in front of me and grabbed the heavy oars. I rowed, the adrenaline pumping through my veins dulling the burning sensation in my muscles. After a long paddle down the thankfully calm moonlit waters, I finally neared the shore of the island. My heart racing, I parked the tiny vessel alongside the dock and hoisted myself out and up the ladder, holding the rope firmly in my hand and securing it to the post. In the darkness, I saw the faint silhouette of our boat tied up mere feet away. The gentle sway of the water pushed it up against the wood, the rhythmic tap the only audible sound besides the water. The sight of it empty caused a lump to form in my throat as I thought of Jack sitting alone in the hospital.

Bat in hand, I retraced our earlier steps while directing the beam of my flashlight to the ground. In the darkness, everything looked eerily different. The already lonesome house seemed even more so with nothing but the faint beam of my light and the glow of the moon to illuminate it. From the neglected yard to the squeaky porch with the spooky looking dolls, everything painted a creepy picture as to what might have gone on in the abandoned house. As I looked around the porch, one thing was for certain: the diary that Jack had come to get earlier was nowhere to be found.

The wind whistled behind me as I opened the loudly creaking door. I tiptoed around, this time examining every nook with my light in hand and keeping an extra eye out for any indication that I wasn't alone. As I moved through the living room, a quick draft of air whiffed behind me as the door slammed shut.

I nearly jumped out of my skin as I instinctively spun around, my heart pounding. Had somebody locked me in or had it merely been the wind? Thankfully, it appeared I was still alone. Hands still shaking, I forced myself deeper into the house, gripping the baseball bat and preparing myself to swing at a moment's notice.

Even though mostly everything was charred, I was still able to see remnants of the décor in the kitchen, a part that I had not yet visited. The dining area had a collapsed table with splinters of broken china and silverware strewn about. I proceeded to an adjacent room, a stately formal dining area blackened from the fire. The sheer amount of dust and ash in the room was nearly unbearable.

Just as I was about to leave, I noticed the ceiling had caved in, leaving a gaping hole between the two floors. I craned my head and shone the flashlight through the opening but couldn't see much. I'd already combed through all the rooms on the first floor of the mansion, so I decided to venture upstairs and cautiously held onto the railing as I slowly ascended the stairs, which, much like the dock, the porch, and everything else I stepped on, creaked beneath my every step.

Not surprisingly, it was even darker on this floor of the house. I proceeded room by room but found nothing of interest, even passing the room with the caved in floor, until I came to the second to last bedroom down the hall. Half of the room was charred, destroyed so badly that the floor had caved in spots. The space was a decent size considering the small bed and petite dresser. Broken toys littered throughout confirmed my hunch that it was a child's room. There was a doll much like the one on the porch lying on the floor that was in near mint condition. Its hair was tied up perfectly in tiny pigtails and it wore a red-checkered dress. When I picked it up, something inside rattled. Curious, I peeked under the doll's dress to find a bell attached to the lanyard that was around its neck.

I frowned. What was it with all the bells around here? I propped the doll up onto the windowsill and began my sweep of the room. Twenty minutes later, I'd been through every drawer, every shelf, and the entire closet. But there was nothing even remotely peculiar; it was a typical child's room in every sense. Here I'd come all the way back hoping to find something—anything— that would clue me in on why someone had attacked Jack. The diary that I knew for a fact I'd left on the table outside was nowhere to be found. Had the person who attacked Jack also taken it?

My final stop was to a door nestled in the corner by the staircase. I figured it was a closet, but when I opened the door and peered inside, I gasped. Before me loomed an enormous library with ceiling high shelves that could only be reached with a ladder.

For a while I simply stood, drinking in the type of room I loved so much. Then, careful not to misplace any of the books, I started from left to right, taking each book off of the shelf and rifling through its pages. Over the next half hour, I had completed my search of nearly four shelves with no luck. I sighed and slumped into a chair. Where in the world was I going to find traces of this house's former owners? Where was the motive behind Jack's attack? The books before me were various types of poetry, guides, and old works of fiction. Nothing out of the ordinary even if they were from another time.

But I was determined. I searched every corner, trying to find something amiss, something incongruent, some sort of clue. I guided the light over each of the shelves, looking for a single discrepancy in the uniform books that lined them. Tucking the flashlight under my arm, I even climbed the ladder to the very tallest shelf, scanning the spines of the books and randomly pulling one out titled *Nations of the World*. As I rifled through its pages, a flutter of papers floated to the floor.

Below me, twenty or so pictures littered the ground. My heart skipped a beat; maybe I'd finally found something. Book still in hand, I carefully descended the steps and scooped up the photos, organizing them face up and by orientation. Then, one by one, I started looking through them. They were all black and white and all of the individuals in the photos wore dated clothing, their faces expressionless save for a few images. One particular photo struck me; it depicted a middle-aged woman with two children, a little boy on her left and a girl on her right. The boy's expression was rigid, his jaw clenched. The mother—or at least I presumed she was the mother—looked serious. Only the little girl looked content as she sat dolled up in her fancy dress. I couldn't tell what it was about the picture that made me feel so strange, but something definitely unnerved me.

The majority of the images showed couples and children with their parents. As I glanced at their faces, I couldn't help but feel their presence around me as I sat in the house I was almost certain they'd lived in. I flipped the photos around hoping to see something written across the back that would give me names to place with the faces but there was nothing. Of the eighteen photos I counted, only one of them—the picture of the woman with the two children—had text scratched across the back, but it wasn't even words. The numbers 9298 were written across the back of the photo. Was it a date perhaps? September 2, 1898?

Giddy at my find, I tucked the photos under my arm and rifled through the book once more. The pages were empty, so I replaced the book on the top shelf exactly where I'd found it and decided I'd had enough of a search for one day. The pictures would give me something to start with, and I wasn't going to leave them for fear that they would meet the same fate the diary had and would not be here upon my return.

Carefully, I proceeded downstairs and out the way I came, wanting nothing more than to get off the island. Something about my time in the house unnerved me; I felt like I was being watched but that was unlikely. Why attack Jack but then let me off scot-free? What century old secret was that house hiding that someone had gone so far as to injure Jack to protect? I didn't know what was going on, but one thing was certain: the story surrounding Herkimer's abandonment had mislead us all and somebody, even a century later, was very much looking to keep it that way. Maybe the house really was haunted; maybe what we were up against wasn't an actual person after all but something totally out of our realm.

I shivered.

Suddenly, a loud flutter sounded behind me.

Tired but instantly propelled by fear, I stumbled out the door and across the lawn. I could feel myself getting weary, my feet dragging like heavy weights.

*Hooo, hooo.*

I stumbled to a halt, my gaze following the sound. The creature's eyes were brighter than fire and staring me in the face. When our eyes locked, it let out its ominous call once more.

The rest of the night's sounds were silent, as though all the creatures of the darkness were still with fear. It seemed as if the owl was trying to warn me, speak to me even, as if it had come here just for me. Maybe it had a message?

*Don't be ridiculous, Meredith.*

But its eyes followed me like a creepy painting, and for some odd reason, I felt mesmerized by it. Its every movement seemed completely in sync with mine, and I nearly jumped out of my skin when it suddenly fluttered its wings and flew away.

What started off as a sluggish trudge across the lawn became a panicked sprint toward safety, despite my knees threatening to give out. The water felt a thousand miles away, and when I finally made it down the dock, I clobbered into the boat. Just as I was positioning the light, I let out a scream.

On the seat in front of me was a bloodied wrench with a small note attached to it.

*For your friend.*

## CHAPTER 10

By the time I made it to the safety of my room, the clock on my nightstand said that it was a little after two in the morning. Although I wanted nothing more than to forget that this day ever happened, I was too shaken up to do anything but lay in bed, wide-eyed, my thoughts in overdrive.

If there had been any doubt in my mind that Jack's injury could have been an accident, I now knew that was not the case. The wrench in my boat was a warning. And while a big part of me wanted to forget we'd ever laid eyes on Herkimer, the other part of me knew I would never be able to let this all go.

The flashing power light of my laptop computer gave me an idea. Maybe, just maybe, I could find something on the Internet about Herkimer. Surely there had to be an article about the wife's sudden death or the house going up in flames.

The fleeting thought was enough that I sleepily stood up. Once at my computer, I typed "Herkimer mansion" into the Internet search field and scrolled down to read the headlines that appeared on my screen.

*Tour opens for General Herkimer's mansion in Mohawk Valley.*

*A history of the Herkimer Diamond Mine.*

*Old home in New York offers rare look inside.*

I sighed; the headlines were clearly not talking about the right house. Over the next hour I clicked page after page of search results with not one single record pertaining to the mansion I was looking for. In this day and age, how could that be? It was as if the house didn't even exist.

I leaned back in my chair, completely discouraged with the dead end. My eyes settled onto the stack of pictures that I had set on the desk, the one on the top of a somber-faced child. I frowned as I held it up to the computer's light. Then, with marked realization, I noticed that behind the chair that the children sat upon was a creepy-faced woman in black trying to conceal herself, almost completely blending in with the background.

* * *

THE BELLS ON the door rattled as I opened it, and Abby and I stepped inside Finnie's. At a round wooden table in the café sat an elderly couple; the husband was reading the newspaper while the wife knit what looked like a blanket. Behind the counter of sweets was a young woman sliding a tray of sugary smelling cookies into the display case.

"They're fresh out of the oven," she said to us with a smile.

My mouth watered. In my rush to visit Jack this morning, I'd completely forgotten to eat breakfast.

115

Now it took all of my self-discipline not to stop to eat first.

Before coming to Finnie's, Abby and I stopped at the hospital only to find Jack peacefully sleeping. We gave him a free pass—9 a.m. *was* early for someone recovering from a head injury. Not wanting to wake him, we carefully retraced our steps out of his room and stopped to talk to the nurse in the hallway. Thankfully, she had good news. Jack's test results had come back normal, and they only had to do one last round of exams before he was discharged this afternoon. She warned that he might experience headaches in the days to come and suggested I make sure he have enough over the counter pain medication to get him through the worst of it. I left my phone number, volunteering to pick him up once he received the all clear.

Now, Abby and I walked right past the sweets, through the café and to the antique shop in the back.

"Hello there," said an eclectic-looking middle-aged woman—she was different than the person who sold me the earring—sitting behind the cashier's desk. Her name tag said Rita, and she was dressed in a colorful orange and purple sundress with one too many pieces of equally rich neon jewelry on her hands, neck, and ears. "How can I help you?"

My agenda for the visit was two-fold. First, there were the jewels that Abby had reminded me we had yet to investigate—we'd opted to keep the gun at Greyhurst for the time being. But tucked away in my purse was also a secret artifact—the picture of the child with the hidden woman in the background and the one with the strange set of numbers on the back that I'd taken from Herkimer. Abby had no knowledge of the photos, so I hoped that I could distract her long enough to ask the questions I so desperately wanted answered. First thing first.

I reached inside my purse and pulled out the velvet bag that held the mysterious jewelry. "I'd like to get some jewelry appraised."

She pulled her bright orange glasses out from atop her curly brown hair and put them on. "Sure, let's see what you've got." She picked up the bag and gently laid all of the pieces onto the glass counter. "That's quite a spread." She chuckled, then raised a concerned eye and looked from me to Abby and back to me. "Please tell me you didn't rob a bank."

I raised my hands in innocence. "No banks were robbed in the collecting of this jewelry. I recently inherited it all," I fibbed. "And before I put it into a safety deposit box, I wanted to get some background on the pieces. I've been told they're antique, but that's about all I know."

Her bangles clamored against the counter as she picked up the emerald bracelet and looked at it with a small magnifier, which she held between her index finger and thumb.

"This one's as real as it gets." She frowned and bent closer to the magnifier, squinting. When she stood back up, she said, "The letters SW are engraved on the inside of this bracelet. Does that mean anything to you?"

She gestured for us to look through the lens. SW. The box had the initials RC. Could it be that this set belonged to a family member with a different surname? I thought of the gun . . . maybe the jewels had been stolen! On the other hand, SW could indicate that they belonged to a member of the Worthington family; that theory also would make sense considering my family owned the property after the Cabots. Why did initials have to be so elusive?

A short while later, Rita replaced all of the pieces back inside the velvet pouch as I tried to come to terms with what we'd learned. Every last piece was authentic and was given a birthday of around 1880, but it was their value that knocked the wind out of my lungs. In the small pouch before me was no less than five million dollars worth of jewels.

"If you want to know more, I'd suggest heading over to the library and looking up pieces from that time. You'll notice a common theme, which could help you identify any other pieces you've got at home."

"Thank you so much! You've been very helpful." My eyes darted to Abby as I wondered how I was going to distract her.

Rita smiled. "Thank you for bringing them in. If you're ever interested in selling, I think I know someone who might be interested. My final word of advice: get those into a safe ASAP. And you probably want to get them insured if they aren't already."

"Most definitely," I reassured her, placing the pouch in my bag. "By any chance, is there a restroom I can use?"

"Just down that way." She gestured toward a door in the far right corner.

I turned to Abby. "I'll only be a few minutes. Want to go grab us a table?"

"Sure, take your time. With all those goodies that I saw walking in, it'll take me forever to figure out what to order."

I waited until she was out of hearing range before I turned back to Rita. "I have another huge favor to ask."

Her eyes sparkled. "Absolutely."

"I came across some photos." I pulled them from my purse and set them down on the table. "On the back of this one there are some numbers written that I wanted to see if you could decipher. But more importantly, I wanted to see if you could tell me why there is a woman hiding in the background of this other one."

She picked up the picture of the child and smiled. "Ah, a hidden mother. Must have been a squirmy child." She pointed to the child's arm. "See that? Looks like the mother was trying to get the little guy to sit still. The long exposures meant anyone being photographed had to sit perfectly still a lot longer than we do today. Plus, don't forget that unsmiling faces and stiff postures were desirable back then. The last thing a parent of that time wanted was a goofy, grinning portrait of their child."

Looking closely, I could see the mother's hand around her son's arm. "How bizarre."

"Let's see this other one," she said, picking up the photo of a different woman with her two young children, each one sitting on a chair on either side of her. Rita studied it intently, then she frowned.

"Oh my," she said at last.

I leaned in to look at it once more. "What is it?"

She looked at me warily, as though wondering if she should reply. "This is a post-mortem photo."

"I'm sorry, what?" But it wasn't hard to guess.

She set the photo down so I could see. "The child in white sitting on her left . . . the one who looks like he's sleeping . . . I'm afraid he's deceased."

I gasped. "How do you know?"

"I know it sounds morbid, but post-mortem pictures were very common in the Victorian ages, especially among infants and young children. Think of it as a way they used to memorialize lost family members. You wouldn't know it immediately from the woman's face because somber expressions were so common anyways, but the fact that the child is so stiff and rigid compared to his sister is a dead giveaway. Plus, although it's a black and white photo, it's clear that the mother is dressed head to toe in black."

I don't think I moved a muscle for several seconds. "I have no idea what to say to that."

"I don't blame you. It can be very disturbing the first time you hear about it." She flipped the photo over. "Now about these numbers . . . I suppose they could be a date, or maybe they were tagged for tracking? A library catalog or archive number maybe?"

My head spun with thoughts completely unrelated to the numbers, and I only half heard what she said. Something about a library?

"Thank you so much for looking at these for me," I finally muttered.

"Anytime. You definitely made my day more interesting!" She rose from her seat and turned to head to the back of the store.

"Wait!" I called out. "Don't I need to pay you?"

She stopped and turned around, chuckling. "No, dear. I do this for fun; call it a hobby of mine."

And with a wink, she was off.

ONCE THE PHOTOS were tucked safely in my purse alongside the jewelry—having such valuable jewels on my person and not safely locked up somewhere made me uneasy—I joined Abby in the café, and we ordered cookies, fudge, and hot chocolate.

"I don't know how much more we'll be able to find out on our own," Abby said as we talked about the initials Rita had found on several, but not all, of the pieces. All of the initials ended with a W, which made us think that they most probably belonged to an old member of the Worthington family. "I'm thinking the right thing to do would be to turn them over to grandmother. Now that we know they're real and most probably belong to our family, there's no way in heck she'd turn them away."

I sipped my hot chocolate, trying my best to stomach it after the explanation of the post-mortem picture. "She'll get them eventually. You do realize that the second we hand them over, we'll never see them again, right? I want to go to the library and do some more research. There has to be a reason why a box so valuable was buried in the garden."

"Fair enough, but can we at least drop them back home before we go? It would be just our luck to get mugged."

The thought of what happened to Jack only recently and the old man I'd been seeing for weeks made me hug the purse tighter to my body. "I couldn't agree more."

LATER THAT AFTERNOON, we made our way to the Hyannis Historical Society library where we spent a good hour looking through the old microfilm archives. To say we made progress was far-fetched; not one single picture with the search criteria Greyhurst and the date range Rita had mentioned showed anyone wearing the jewels.

"We need to refine our search," I said at last. "Greyhurst and every synonym known to mankind for the word party has gotten us nowhere."

Abby chewed her lip. "What about looking up Worthington and removing Greyhurst? I'm sure there were parties hosted at other locations. If that doesn't work, we could look into our family tree and see if we can match up the initials with the dates."

"It's worth a shot," I said as I updated the filters.

Searching for the surname Worthington turned up more results than I knew what to do with. I was interested in the pictures, so I filtered by images only and we went one by one.

"Jackpot," Abby said as we landed on a black-and-white sketched image of a woman wearing an intricate evening gown and elaborate jewelry. Her hand was gently placed over the arm of the man beside her, and I zoomed the image in to look at her ring.

"That's the garnet set all right." I scrolled down and proceeded to read the text aloud. "July 21, 1879, Mr. and Mrs. Clyde Worthington attend musical at the Institute Hall."

"So the Worthingtons have been partying it up for well over a hundred years," Abby joked.

"Probably a lot longer. I'm going to remove the date filter and see what comes back. If I sort by oldest first we can see just how long this crazy family has been at it." I sent the image to print and went back to the search screen.

A few quick clicks later, and a whole new set of results populated the screen. Before I could even sort them, an image icon caught my eye. Although small, it showed an unmistakable sea of white, the kind that only a wedding picture would have. I clicked it.

Abby stiffened beside me as we both stared at the picture of my mother and father on their wedding day. They could have passed as royalty. Easily. My mother wore a long-sleeved, poofy-bottomed gown with a lace veil pinned to her blonde hair, which was twisted into an elegant up-do. My father looked like a younger version of his present-day self; he wore a tuxedo, looked about twenty pounds thinner, and had a head full of medium brown hair.

What stood out most was the instantly recognizable happiness etched upon their faces. Smiles as big as theirs I had never, ever seen before.

I wasn't sure why, but seeing the pictures affected me in ways that I couldn't in that moment explain. I abruptly stood, unable to bear looking at that photo any longer.

"I need to get out of here," I said to Abby. Then I spun on my heels, leaving the images plastered on the screen behind me, the eerie feeling of being watched by my parents staying with me until I was out of the library.

# CHAPTER 11

"Pick up, Jack, please," I pleaded out loud. But I got his voicemail again. I reluctantly stabbed the end button and looked at the long trail of times I'd tried calling him. Unless something was wrong, he should have been released from the hospital by now. Where *was* he?

I shoved the phone into my pant pocket and stared mindlessly out at the water. Even the dock on which I now stood wasn't far enough away from Greyhurst, wasn't far enough from the very place my mother stood looking so happy in the picture that was ingrained in my mind.

*Ding!*

My phone chimed loudly, and my heart nearly leapt out of my chest. I retrieved my cell with shaky hands, and it almost slipped from my grasp. It was from Jack.

*Don't turn around*, it said.

I wrote back. *Why not? Where are you?*

*You'll know in a second.*

Butterflies burst to life inside my stomach. It seemed like forever until footsteps shuffled behind me. My legs suddenly felt like dead weights, and I couldn't have moved them if I tried. My breath caught in my chest as the footsteps grew more pronounced. For the first time in my life, I felt an indescribable zing of energy between us, like an invisible charge was pulling us closer. Suddenly it was silent except for the rhythmic flow of the waves. I took a deep breath.

Before my mind could register what I knew was going to happen, Jack's hand slid into mine. In that instant, my jaw unclenched and my tense body relaxed. My palm instantly tingled, an electric current flowing between his hand and mine. All at once, every ounce of anger and disappointment I'd harbored toward my mother felt as if it had never existed. All at once, it was the farthest thing from my mind. Jack was okay, and in this moment that was all that mattered.

I quietly savored his hand in mine for a few seconds longer before turning towards him, and in an instant my happiness burst like a bubble of dew falling to the ground.

"Hello," he said gently.

I tried not to grimace when I registered how tired he looked. Dark circles were prominent below his now swollen eyes. Around his head was a white bandage.

"Oh, Jack," was all I could say. Tears pricked my eyes—whether they were happy tears or sad tears, I was not sure.

"I'm okay, I promise. It looks worse than it is." He reached for my other hand and held both up to his chest. Then he took a deep breath. "I know I said it before but I want you to promise me again that you'll never go back to Herkimer. I want to put that crazy place behind us. I should have listened to you that first day we met . . . that place is no joke, and I'm sorry I ever put you in danger."

"You didn't—" I began, guilt at having broken my word and gone back washing over me. What good had it been? Not only had I concealed the truth from Abby and lied to Jack but seeing Herkimer only left me with more questions than I'd started with. "I promise, I'm done. I will never step foot on that island again."

Somehow, talking released the floodgates that held my emotions at bay, and now I felt as though I was drowning once more.

"What's wrong?" Jack asked, his furrowed brow crinkling his bandage. "Did I upset you?"

"No," I said quickly. "I'm sorry."

He lifted my chin, and our eyes locked. "You can tell me what's wrong. You can tell me anything, Meredith."

I nodded, and a few long seconds passed before the words I wanted to say bubbled to the surface. "I feel so lost, Jack. I have so many emotions running through me I don't even know where to start. Above everything though, I can't get over the guilt that I feel around you getting injured."

"There is no way we could have known I would get attacked, Meredith. For all we thought, we were trespassing on a deserted island. We obviously went too far and there were consequences. So long as we don't go back, there's no reason anything else should happen. We never took anything; if there's a silver lining to you forgetting the journal, that's it."

But I had taken something, I thought remorsefully, thinking of the creepy photos.

"Is that all that's bothering you?" Jack asked after I stayed silent.

I decided to steer the subject away from Herkimer and confess the other thing weighing on my mind.

"Abby and I have been looking into the jewelry we found in the box and let's just say one search led to another and I somehow stumbled across a picture of my mother at their wedding here at Greyhurst. She looked . . . she looked *happy*." I paused to look back at Greyhurst, imagining the wedding party in action before my eyes.

"Anyone else would have been excited to find such a picture. But how can I be? My entire family hates her. Do you know I've never been allowed to ask a single question about why she left? I tried once when I was little, and my grandmother made me swear never to mention her again. She said that everyone makes choices, and that my mother had made hers, that I should move on and appreciate what I did have: more wealth than most people would ever lay eyes on. Like I even cared then or now. She never said be thankful you have a loving family or a loving father; it was all about the money. Which is why looking at my mother so happy in that picture made me even more confused on why she'd leave. She had had financial security *and* love, why leave? Maybe she didn't love me the way she did my father? Maybe I was the reason she left." Tears were flowing down my cheeks and I was a mess, a pathetic puddle of emotions.

Jack gripped my hands. "That is *not* why she left. Couples change, Meredith. I've seen it happen to my friends' parents, to members of my family. I've seen people who were so in love grow to absolutely hate one another. It's sad and it doesn't always make sense, but sometimes the unimaginable does happen."

I took a step back and looked at him. "I just wish I knew what happened. I'm tired of pretending that I don't wonder about her. And I'm tired of feeling like I *shouldn't* be wondering about her, even though it's clear no one else does. I'm tired of people whispering about her and my father when they think no one's listening . . . I don't see how people can throw dangerous assumptions out there like it's nothing," I said, thinking back to the conversation I overheard amongst my grandmother's guests.

"You need to talk to your father, Meredith. Regardless of what the rest of your family says, I'm sure he's been expecting this conversation for years. He's had enough time to make peace with it that he won't turn you away; he's the only one who can help you get closure. You owe it to yourself not to spend a lifetime questioning."

Hearing it from Jack only solidified what I already knew. I'd been dancing around this topic for as long as I could remember, and I sensed that my father had been, too. I would be the bigger one, I decided. If I waited around for him to feel it was the right time, I would probably be middle aged and he on his deathbed, if it happened even then.

"Thank you," I said. "For being here for me."

He didn't say anything, but I felt his hands give me a reassuring squeeze before I pulled back.

"Hey, they were supposed to call me to pick you up. How did you—"

"I didn't want to bother you—you've already done so much just getting me to the hospital. I felt fine so I called a taxi." Despite how reassured he sounded earlier about how the threat of Herkimer was now behind us, his voice cracked and I saw a glint of hesitation in his eyes as he quickly glanced away from me and settled his gaze on Herkimer. My own stomach dropped not just out of fear for the forces working against us, but that they might somehow stand in the way of developing feelings we both knew couldn't be stopped.

LATER THAT NIGHT, the butterflies were still in full force, only this time the reason was two-fold. On the one hand, I could still smell Jack's cologne, could feel his hands around mine. On the other, I was filled with apprehension at the idea of talking candidly with my father. What had seemed like a great idea when I was with Jack now petrified me in my aloneness.

Abby was passed out cold a few rooms down, and for the last hour I'd been tossing and turning in my bed, wide-awake as ever. I sighed and pulled the crisp sheets up to my chin, and then I stretched out as far as my legs would go before curling up to my pillows. No matter what I tried, I just couldn't get comfortable. The time on my alarm clock read a little after eleven-thirty, and I knew that slumber was wishful thinking.

Reading usually helped lull me into a calm enough state of mind that I could doze. Sensing that it would help—and knowing I could use all the help I could get—I forced myself out of bed, grabbed my fluffy white bathrobe, and staggered down the hall.

When I reached the library, the door was slightly ajar, a faint trail of light streaming out into the dark hallway. I peered into the opening, squinting as my eyes adjusted to the bright lights. Inside were two people standing by the ceiling-high window that was opened to the night sky. The first person I recognized as my father. From the balding spot on the back of his head and his slightly heavier build, I knew the second was Arthur's. Both were dressed in suits and their backs were toward me. And both appeared to be standing so rigidly that they did not so much as flinch as they gazed out the window.

I quietly sat outside the door. It was rare that I got to witness a private conversation between father and his most trusted companion, and my curiosity got the best of me.

"I don't know what to do, this time the threat is simply too great—" I barely heard my father whisper as he continued to stare out the window.

Arthur's father replied. "We're doing everything we can," I heard him say. "Are you sure it's—"

Suddenly, footsteps tapped in the distance. I froze, completely missing what Arthur's father had said. Are you sure it's *what*? But the footsteps were getting closer by the second. Careful not to make a sound, I slowly stood and gave one last peek inside to make sure they had not heard me. Then I lightly sprinted in the opposite direction back down the hall.

Once in my room, I stood by the doorway, laying my head on the door as I listened to my heart beating wildly. The mood in the library seemed so tense. My father always carried himself formally around his staff, but not Arthur's father.

I turned off my light and hastily ran to bed, scurrying back in and covering myself up as though to shield myself from the unknown peril that lurked in my dark bedroom. I disliked the darkness of my room when I was alone and wished Abby was with me, especially after what I had just heard. As I lay, I tried to think happier thoughts, tried to think of my earlier encounter with Jack and my ever-increasing feelings for him, knowing full well that I would never fall asleep in this state of mind. I wanted to call him, but knew he was sleeping; in his last text, he said how exhausted he was, and how could I blame him? He'd only just been released from the hospital.

Plus, there were still too many questions that I needed answered, and the only way I would have any peace of mind was if I had an honest, completely open conversation with my father like Jack had suggested. There was simply no getting around that.

I flipped onto my side and stared, my eyes wide with fright, out the window into the darkness, until eventually my eyelids got heavy and I fell asleep.

*TAKE A DEEP breath*, I commanded myself before knocking on the heavy wooden door.

"Come in," I heard my father call.

I pushed the door open and entered the library. "Good morning, father."

It was 9 a.m., and he was already dressed for the day and sitting at the large wooden desk with the day's newspaper, a cup of coffee, and a pastry.

"Dear, sweet Meredith. I have missed you so much." He rose, a smile on his face, and walked toward me.

Feeling his affectionate arm around my shoulder made me temporarily forget why I'd come. He sounded so carefree and happy to see me that all of a sudden I wondered if I was just being overly paranoid by wanting to have this conversation.

"How are you? Tell me what you've been up to this summer," he asked.

I took a seat across from him in a stately antique chair emblazoned with the Worthington family crest that was situated in front of the desk. "I'm all right. I, uh, had something I wanted to talk to you about—if you've got time."

"Of course." He returned to his chair, sat down, and looked at me expectantly.

My heart skipped a beat. "First, I wanted to see how the campaign is going . . . "

He sipped his coffee. "Aside from the threats to expose what the opposing party thinks is dirty laundry, it's been great. Campaigns open up all sorts of information, from the time that the firm got audited to the recording that aired at the gala. There's a lot of damage control being done, nothing major."

The ladies of Hyannis Port certainly didn't help quell rumors about him, but I wasn't going to mention their gossip. My father reacted with such nonchalance that I decided to move on to the more pressing topic.

"I've been thinking a lot about my mother lately." The words spilled from my mouth. "I found a picture of you both on your wedding day. Seeing it made me realize just how little I know about her . . . How did you meet? What was she like? But I guess what I want to know most of all is why she would leave. How can someone who once looked so happy leave?"

My father paled, staring at me with unblinking eyes. This was the conversation that he'd been putting off for years, and I imagined he was uncomfortable, but the time had come that we talk about it once and for all.

He swallowed, then his back straightened and he cleared his throat. "I suppose I should start at the beginning," he said. "Your mother and I met one spring in the library at Harvard. I was finishing up my first year of law school, and would you believe I had yet to even step foot in the campus library?" He had a small smile on his face as he gazed at one of the bookshelves in Greyhurst's library. "As you can imagine, I looked like a fish out of water. I had a thirty-page paper due the next morning . . . something about corporate law . . . and for some crazy reason, I left it for the last minute. Lillian saw me wandering the aisles, and like the true book lover that she was, she offered to help me find what I was looking for. I still remember how she graciously set down the stack of books she'd been carrying—she was an art history major and had her own paper due—and helped me locate the section on law. When she found out my paper was due the next day, she insisted we sit at a table and get to work. We stayed in the library all night—me writing, while she kept track of the hundreds of sources I'd cited. Just before the sun came up, I was done."

I listened to his story, soaking in every word.

"You'd never know she'd been up all night the way she energetically rose and gathered her books. 'The library is going to be your best friend these next few years. Don't be so scared of it,' she teased as she walked away. Thinking back on it now, I don't know why I didn't get her last name or her number. It was only as I sat in class that morning that I realized how much I owed her a thank you; I would've failed if I hadn't finished that paper. I guess it's not hard to see that I was a little arrogant back then. I had the whole *people serve me, I don't serve people* type of attitude that I'd seen my own parents have. That afternoon, I went over to the Art department and there, in one of the hallways, was a picture of her on the wall. Lillian Greene. She was the president of the Art History club that met every Monday and Wednesday during lunch. I swallowed my pride and went to the next meeting, and I guess you can say the rest is history. Your mother changed me. She made me a better person and brought me back down to earth. She was so humble that, for the first time in my life, I felt ashamed at who I was."

He lowered his head and took a deep breath.

"We'd been going out for months before we drove to Greyhurst for Thanksgiving. It was the first time she'd seen me out of the dorms, in my real element. I'm only glad she got to know the real me before all of this." He waved his hand around the room.

"We were married that Christmas Eve, a lovely ceremony here at Greyhurst. It was snowing, practically a blizzard, but she was a trooper and never lost her cool once. Even when the cake froze and nobody ate it. Our honeymoon lasted a little less than a week; we had to be back for the new semester. Those first few years of our marriage were far from conventional. We were students and I, heeding her advice, spent almost all of my free time at the library. Thankfully she had no qualms about tagging along; she could spend hours lost in the shelves. The spring that I graduated law school was the same spring we found out she was pregnant. We were technically homeless, having finally moved out of the dorms, and decided that moving to Greyhurst so I could practice with your grandfather would make sense while we took our time to figure out where we wanted to start our family. She had a great pregnancy, and you arrived on time that December."

I swallowed as I saw the look on his face turn somber.

"I don't know what happened that winter, but something about Lillian changed. She was depressed; it could have been anything—postpartum, the cold, lonely winter at Greyhurst. I was so busy with my work, with trying to prove to your grandfather that I was worthy of inheriting his legacy, that I was absent a lot of the time. It couldn't have been easy for her. Your grandmother had her area socialites, but your mother never cared much for that scene." He gave me a pleading glance. "It was a rough patch in our marriage for sure. We argued a lot; I should have seen those fights for what they were: her desperate attempts to show me that she was nearing the end of her fight. Your grandfather officially transferred the practice to me that following spring. There was a huge celebratory party here. I remember how beautiful she looked getting you dressed for the event; she always looked so content holding you. It was the only time I saw true happiness from her those last few months, when she was doting on you. It was the last night I ever saw her . . . you were tucked into your bassinet with the nanny when I finally came to bed in the wee hours of the morning, assuming she was asleep. There was a letter on her side of the bed. 'I can no longer pretend' was her opening line, and it was that night that her message of the last few months became clear: that I was the reason she left."

Goosebumps prickled my skin as he said those words. That explained so much of his mood over the years. It even explained why I felt like he avoided me on certain occasions, why the sheer sight of me was painful—he obviously harbored guilt over being the reason I had no mother. But I chose not to comment. Instead, I silently reflected. What my father said made perfect sense. I could hardly stand Greyhurst for the summer—and I had Abby. Surely a newlywed and new mother who was all alone would be tempted to leave. The only thing I didn't understand was why she didn't take me with her.

"I understand if you blame me," my father said. "I still blame myself; it was one of the biggest mistakes of my life."

"Didn't you try to find her? To make it up to her?" My voice cracked. If he had, I might still have my mother today.

"I searched for months, but she did not want to be found. The letter that she wrote before she left explicitly said not to go after her. I could have involved the authorities, but why force someone to come back? She knew where to find us if she had a change of heart. The day I decided to stop searching was the hardest day of my life." He squeezed his eyes shut for several long moments. "You have to understand that the family felt betrayed after she ran away. I admit, I felt betrayed, too, but I have also blamed myself for years. Your grandparents felt like they'd given her the world and couldn't forgive her for tarnishing their name. With time, emotions eventually fade, Meredith, but I'm not sure that any of us will ever truly forget. Most important, though, is that you know that this was never about you. She probably, in some strange way, figured she was doing this *for* you. She would never have wanted you to be exposed to her unhappiness."

There were so many emotions drifting around in my head that I knew I shouldn't let them get the better of me. In my heart, I knew he was right, that she was an adult woman who'd made a conscious decision—even if he was the cause, how could I blame him for a choice that she'd ultimately made? But something he said in our discussion suddenly rang in my mind.

*It was one of the biggest mistakes of my life.*

What else did I not know?

## CHAPTER 12

The next day, I awoke to the ringing of my cell phone. Jack's name flashed across the screen, and I answered quickly, scared that something might be wrong.

I cleared my throat, trying to get rid of my groggy morning voice. "Hello?"

"I woke you up, didn't I?"

"No, not at all." I peeked over at my bedside alarm clock and saw that it was just shy of nine in the morning. Jack sounded like he'd been awake for hours. "What's going on?"

"Well, I know it's early, but I was just heading out to this farm to get some plants for the new entryway landscape, and I was wondering if you would like to join me. Abby is welcome to join too of course."

Not sure why he'd want us to go to a farm—what was there to do?—and still quite sleepy, it took me a few seconds to process his invitation.

"You there?" he asked.

"Yeah, I'm here, sorry," I said quickly. I propped myself up in my bed. "Sure, we'll come."

"Great, I'll pick you up in a bit."

After hanging up the phone, I quickly showered and threw on some jeans, a tank top, and sneakers. Then I went to find Abby, who said that despite the kind offer, she would much prefer to get more sleep than to traipse around in manure. Couldn't say that I blamed her; had it not been an outing with Jack, I would have felt the same.

Abby clearly suspected the dynamic between Jack and I had started to change and I couldn't help but wonder if this was her secret attempt to give us our space. What started out as playful jests had recently turned into meaningful questions on how I felt about Jack. And her being my closest friend meant that I told her exactly how I felt, including my fears that my father would disapprove and my apprehension that the end of summer would mean an end to a meaningful friendship that I desperately wanted to last.

When I reached Greyhurst's parking lot, Jack was standing beside his blue Jeep, and the butterflies in my stomach went wild. He looked so handsome in his blue cargo shorts and tight V-neck T-shirt.

"Have you been here long?" I asked as I walked up to his car. "I'm sorry to keep you waiting."

He smiled. "Not long at all. Where's Abby?"

"Getting her beauty sleep. Looks like it's just the two of us."

He opened the car door for me. I climbed in, the faint trace of Jack's aftershave making me feel mildly intoxicated.

He hopped in and reversed out of the driveway. The farm, he said, wasn't far from Greyhurst. "I'm sorry to wake you up, I thought you would like this place and . . . and I missed you."

I felt my cheeks flush. I hadn't seen Jack in over a day, which suddenly felt like a lifetime. "I missed you, too," I said.

He continued down the winding roads, and finally I broke the silence, "I did it, you know."

Jack turned to me, and a knowing smile crossed his face. "You talked to him?"

I nodded. "I'm so glad I listened to you." After filling him in on what I'd learned, I said, "I never thought I'd say this, but I really do forgive my family for not wanting to talk about it, it couldn't have been easy for either side. And although it will take me a while to fully comprehend my mother's decision, I think I can let it go for a while. Thank you for your advice; I don't think I would have mustered the courage without you."

"I'm really happy you're able to put this topic behind you. It couldn't have been easy."

"You have no idea," I muttered.

About ten minutes later, Jack parked on the grass outside of a white wooden fence lining an endless expanse of trees. Once again, he came to my side of the car and graciously opened the door for me.

As we walked beyond the fence, I was amazed at the greenery that surrounded us; unlike Greyhurst, the ocean was nowhere to be found. I gazed upwards, amazed that the bright blue, unblemished sky was virtually covered by the canopies of leaves that the concentration of trees created.

"It almost feels like we're in a different state," I marveled. "I'm used to sand and seagulls."

"It kind of does, doesn't it?" he said. I watched him scan our surroundings, a frown suddenly forming at his brows.

"What is it?" I asked.

"It's going to rain."

I stared at him incredulously. "Rain? What do you mean? The weather is amazing!"

He gestured towards a herd of cattle on the grass in the distance. "See those cows? They're sitting down, which means it's going to rain. My great-grandmother always used to say that when the cows sit, it means rain is near. She was never wrong."

"No offense to your great-grandmother but today has to be the exception," I said. "There is not a single cloud in the sky."

He grinned. "We'll see about that."

As we headed deeper into the woods, I could see why Jack didn't mind coming here. From what I'd come to learn about his hometown, this seemed like what he'd grown up with: tranquility, nature, the great outdoors. Or, in other words, the complete antithesis of my upbringing.

Once we reached the tiny shed in the middle of the fenced area, I saw two older individuals sitting on a wooden bench.

"Jack!" the man said, giving Jack a loving pat on the shoulder. He was lanky and wore a faded brown jacket, jeans, and a cowboy hat. Sunspots dotted his face, white hair and a white mustache accentuating his tan skin tone. "I'm so glad you could make it, son."

Jack turned to me. "Meredith, this is John. He owns the farm."

"How do you do, ma'am?" John asked, tipping his cowboy hat as he spoke.

"I'm fine, thank you," I replied, humbled by his gracious welcome.

Jack then greeted the grey-haired woman by John's side. "And this is his wife, Mary."

Mary rose to hug Jack, the apron she wore over her beige capris and yellow shirt dusted with flour.

She patted my shoulder and, with the most welcoming smile, said, "It's great to have you here."

"Thank you, I'm happy to be here," I replied, realizing just how much I meant those words.

"And this—" Jack walked over to a caramel-colored horse tied to its stable. "This is Chestnut." He patted her golden mane, untied her, and handed me the rope. "You ready to take her out for a ride?"

My eyes widened. "Really? I would love to!"

He smiled. "Then up we go," he said as he took my hand, and I stepped up onto the stirrup and got comfortably seated. "I'll be right back."

I stroked the mare's neck as I watched him talk to John, who stood with the other horse, a pretty chocolate brown mare. Much to my surprise, instead of mounting his own horse, Jack made his way back to me while John led the horse back into the stable.

"I hope you don't mind, but it appears that Cocoa over there doesn't feel much like riding." The mischievous sparkle in his eye gave his lie away.

"Poor Cocoa," I indulged. "I guess Chestnut had better brace herself."

With a chuckle and a quick step up, Jack was seated behind me, his arms framing mine as he held my hands and we both gripped the reins. Feeling his skin against mine once more sent a jolt up my spine and I felt exhilarated by the intimacy of our contact. It all seemed like a scene in a movie. Girl and boy meet and develop feelings for one another. They take long strolls by the water whispering sweet nothings. They spend hours talking and can't imagine going a day without speaking. Why, to do so would be hell on earth. But that's where the movies usually went one of two ways. A lump of apprehension formed in my throat. There was virtually no way my family would support my association with Jack—as a friend or otherwise. But I wouldn't think about that today, I resolved.

I nudged the horse gently, and we were on our way. Although I hadn't ridden in a while—I had taken horseback riding lessons throughout my childhood and had been trained by the best equestrians in the nation—surprisingly all my teachings seemed to come flooding back. Before long, Chestnut was trotting out the white fences.

"I'm impressed," Jack said. "You're quite a natural."

"Shhhh," I commanded. "My riding instructor always said you don't ever credit a rider when a horse is nearby. They understand and don't appreciate not receiving any praise."

I felt Jack's laugh reverberate behind me. "You have my sincerest apologies, Chestnut. Meredith is a horrible rider, I was only trying to feed her ego."

"That's better," I said with a chuckle.

We had reached a clearing, so I nudged Chestnut into a gallop. "Hang on," I said to Jack.

He gripped my waist a little tighter.

"I forgot to tell you I've never ridden before!" he said loudly over the sound of Chestnut's hooves.

I glided her to a gentle stop. "You're joking," I said, looking at him over my right shoulder.

I could tell he was trying to keep a straight face. "Jack!" I said, playfully hitting him on the thigh.

He burst into laughter. "Of course I'm joking."

At my command, Chestnut started walking once more.

"I hope you're having fun," Jack said quietly from behind me.

I turned my head again and smiled. "More than you know."

"Good." He hugged his arms around me. "I'm not sure how much longer you'll be in town, but I hope I can come see you after I start school in the fall. I'll drive as far as I have to to see you. That is, if you want me to."

Rapturous emotion swallowed my heart whole. "I would love that."

"I worry, though, that your family might not like the idea of you spending time with me."

The words hung between us. As much as we cared to deny it, we came from two vastly different worlds.

"It's no one's decision who I spend my time with but my own," I said resolutely.

"I know, I just don't want to cause you any problems. And I don't just mean with your family . . . I'm not ignorant as to our differences and I want to make sure you're comfortable with this . . . with us."

I gave his hand a pat. "You have nothing to worry about."

We continued to ride until, eventually, we reached the outskirts of the property and turned back. Birds of all different kinds chirped and flew about through the beautiful rays of light streaming between the leaves of the forest canopy. I felt as though I had been placed into the majestic scenery of a storybook. As we approached the stable, I heard the faint noise of a bell ringing coming from the quaint little house in the distance.

"You're just in time," John said as we approached. "Food's ready. Mary hates it when her food gets cold, so I'll let you two head inside while I put Chestnut back."

Jack jumped down and offered his hand to help me. "I forgot to mention that they have generously invited us to join them for lunch. You don't mind, do you?"

"Not at all," I replied, wondering if this day could possibly get any better.

As chance would have it, just as we started walking towards the house, a light drizzle began to fall from the sky.

JACK DROPPED ME off at Greyhurst a few minutes shy of two o'clock. Thankfully, the rain hadn't lasted long—just a light summer shower—but much to Jack's delight, it did indeed prove his great-grandmother's theory.

Lunch had been heavenly; the spread of comfort food that Mary put out was such a far cry from the types of food I'd been eating as of late that I think I ate enough for a family of four. My grandmother would be mortified.

Carrying a wrapped plate of food for Abby—Mary had insisted—I couldn't wait to find her and tell her about Jack's surprise. If she really was trying to give us our space, well, she couldn't have chosen a better day to do it.

At the side door, I paused to readjust the things I was carrying, and nearly jumped out of my skin when someone called, "Care to challenge us to a match?"

Arthur. I would know that voice anywhere.

I looked up to see him standing on the tennis court, clad in shorts and a shirt that was now stuck to his skin, his brow glistening with sweat. And to my jaw-dropping surprise, Abby was standing opposite of him dressed head to toe in tennis attire, a racket in hand.

When I didn't move, the door to the court swung open, and Arthur strode toward me, Abby following suit. "Come on, you know you want to."

I raised a curious eyebrow and set my purse and the plate of food down on a bench. "First of all, where on earth have you been these days?" I placed my hands on my hips. "And how on earth did you get Abby to play with you?"

He smirked. "First of all, I don't know what you mean. And second of all, how could she resist this?" He gestured to himself, and I rolled my eyes.

Abby strode up beside him, her face as red as her hair. I picked up the plate. "I brought you homemade macaroni and cheese, chicken pot pie, and blueberry crumble. Sorry, Arthur, I didn't know you'd be here."

Her answer came out in short pants. "That's . . . so . . . nice . . . of . . . you. I'm starving—" She picked up the plate and took it a few feet away to a picnic table overlooking the tennis court.

"So you'll play?" Arthur asked, one eyebrow raised.

"Under one condition," I answered.

"Name your price."

"You need to tell me what the hell went on that day we went to Herkimer and why you've been acting so strange ever since." I watched him closely and, sure enough, his face became a few shades paler.

"I already told you, nothing happened."

I crossed my arms. "I take it Abby didn't tell you what happened to Jack?"

His eyebrows knit closer together, and for a brief moment, I felt relieved. I had no idea who else besides Arthur could have known that we'd go back to

Herkimer, and the inevitable seed of doubt that had crossed my mind had bugged me for days.

"What happened to Jack?" Arthur asked.

My jaw clenched as I recalled the story of the day Jack got attacked. "So now you see why I want to know. And why you are going to tell me."

Arthur swallowed, his unspoken nervousness palpable. My heart skipped a beat. I'd been going on an assumption. But now it was clear to me that he knew something—I was certain.

"It's nothing," he said, but he sounded like he was trying to convince himself just as much as he was me.

"Arthur," I said firmly.

He took a couple steps closer until he was only a few inches away from me and, in a low voice, said, "I don't want to hurt you . . . "

That was definitely not what I was expecting to hear. "What do you mean *hurt me*, Arthur?"

"Please, just believe me, if I thought it had anything to do with Jack's injury, I would tell you, but this is an entirely different ballgame."

My curiosity piqued—not just because of what happened to Jack, but because it sounded like what Arthur knew had to do with me, and I couldn't, for the life of me, imagine what it could be. "Arthur, whatever it is, I need you to tell me. *Please.*"

He exhaled and looked away as he said the following words: "I found something that day at Herkimer, Meredith, and I believe it belonged to your mother."

The world around me spun in dizzying circles as I tried to comprehend what he'd said. "You . . . you found something of my mother's?" My voice shook. "But . . . how do you know? What was it?"

He looked me square in the eye. "The day we went to Herkimer, when I went off to look on my own, I wandered into one of the rooms and saw something sticking out from under the bed. When I bent down and picked it up, I saw that it was a program from a party and it had your mother's name on it. Lillian Worthington. It had some numbers on it, but they made no sense. I had no idea what that party was, so I started doing some research, and this is where I didn't want to have to tell you this . . . The program that I found was from the party on the night that your mother was last seen."

"You're sure?" I asked.

He fumbled around in the gym bag that was on the bench, pulled out a picture, and handed it to me. "I just found this yesterday. This was what your mother was wearing the night that she disappeared. This is a picture from the party, and if you look at her hands, you'll see that she was carrying the program."

I looked at the picture of my mother. It was a side shot—a candid shot—of her talking to another party goer, a woman who looked to be about her age who was also dressed in a floor length gown. My mother's was blue with an elegant cream-colored lace pattern in the upper bodice, and she looked as regal as royalty. In her hand, she held a piece of paper.

"How do you know that this is the same program?" I asked.

Arthur pulled out another picture and handed it to me. This one showed only the program in her hand, which clearly showed her name elegantly written across the top. "I had that picture enlarged. I had a hunch it was the same thing, but I needed proof."

I looked at him, unblinking, trying to comprehend what all this meant. "So . . . if she was at the party, then how did her program get to Herkimer?"

"That's what I've been wondering."

I took a deep breath. The more I thought about it, the more I realized that I should have made the connection. Nothing good had ever happened at Herkimer. From the very start, it had been filled with stories of loss and devastation.

"Arthur . . . I've always secretly wondered if—" I stopped mid-sentence, realizing that to finish it would reveal something that I wasn't sure I was ready to admit out loud. But it needed to be said. Now more than ever. "I've always had the gut feeling that my mother didn't run away."

His face turned to stone. "You wouldn't be the only one. And I think I know how we can find out."

## CHAPTER 13

Moments later, Abby and I were sitting in Arthur's Audi coupe, and he was speeding out the gates of Greyhurst.

"What is so urgent that you wouldn't even let me go inside and pee?" Abby asked as her eyes bore into the side of Arthur's face. He was expertly shifting his sports car into gear, the speed nearly pinning me into my seat.

"I'll tell you when we get there," he said.

She rolled her eyes. "And how, might I ask, did you stumble upon this thing that we just *have* to see? You've got to do better than that."

"I'll tell her," I said to Arthur, then proceeded to fill Abby in.

"That doesn't make any sense," Abby whispered. "Why would your mother have been at Herkimer?"

Arthur shifted uncomfortably. "If I had to guess, I'd say that this family has an enemy who has been using Herkimer's proximity to keep a close watch on you all," he said firmly as he stared at the road ahead. "I've heard the whispers about your father's campaign. I'm not sure what you've been told, but somebody out there is posing a real threat to his li—uh, reputation."

"The old man," I said without even realizing the words had escaped my lips. Then I told them of all the times I'd seen him and how, from the beginning, I felt as if he'd been up to something.

My mind in overdrive, I leaned back in my seat and stared at the passing trees. As much as I now despised Arthur for withholding this for so long, I realized that it had probably come at the instruction of my father who I knew wouldn't want me aware of the threat.

What, besides the gaffe at the gala, had gone on? Arthur said that his reputation—

Suddenly, I turned to him in blatant astonishment. "You meant to say there was a threat to my father's life, didn't you?"

He took a deep breath but didn't say anything.

I blinked, shifting back. "Arthur John Proctor, you tell me right now!"

"I wish I knew more. I only overheard my father mention something in passing," he said warily.

So that's why Arthur's father had been at our house! Tears filled my eyes. "Who would want to harm him just because of a stupid election?"

"First of all, I'm pretty sure the reason goes beyond the election. I have a hunch that there's some sort of tie to Herkimer, but for the life of me, I can't figure it out. But either way, your father has a lot to be envied. He is smart, successful, wealthy—and it only keeps getting better, which is more than a lot of people can say. The election was probably the tipping point, the icing on the cake if you will."

"How are we ever going to find out who's behind it all?"

"First we need to see if we can figure out what happened to your mother." He stopped at a red light and turned to look at me. From just beyond, I could see a tall stone church with a bright red door and tall stained glass windows. "You aren't going to like this."

"What do you mean?" I asked uneasily.

He reached for my hand. "If your family really did lie about what happened to your mother, I think this would give us a definitive answer."

I gulped as he pulled up to the parking lot of the church, which was bustling with cars, a hearse confirming why there were so many people on a weekday. As the car came to a halt, Arthur moved the shift into park and powered off the engine.

The grey walls of the church were aged, the stone covered in spots with bright green ivy. The mourners were still gathered inside, which I was thankful for because I hardly looked as though I belonged at a funeral with what I was wearing.

"Are we going inside?" Abby asked.

"No, we're going to the cemetery."

I was still sitting frozen in my seat when he came around and opened my car door.

"You have got to be kidding me," I said as I stepped out into the sunlight.

"Nope, not kidding."

"Holy crap," Abby muttered as we walked through the parking lot to the church, her arm looped in mine.

We proceeded past the church to the right side of the building where the old cemetery was. Paper-thin tombstones formed zigzagged lines in the grass. Many of them were bent and a few were broken, but all of them looked pretty much identical. We walked past several rows of graves and sculpted angels until we reached a medium-sized old stone building in the center of the graveyard that had WORTHINGTON engraved in large bold letters above the entryway. It was a mausoleum.

"Grandmother did mention something about our family plot being here," I recalled.

"Do me a favor and look out for anybody coming while I go to the back and pick the lock," Arthur instructed.

I stepped in his way. "Are you insane? You can't break into a mausoleum!"

He threw his hands up in the air. "It's either that or we walk right into the memorial service and ask the priest for the key. Look, you see that plaque?" He gestured to a framed rectangle on the stone wall. "Both of your parents' names are on it. Call it planning for the future—or not. Don't you think your family would have seen to it that your mother's name was removed if she'd run off?"

I looked at the tablet on the wall of the edifice and shuddered. My mother's name was indeed carved into the stone. But so were my grandparents' and my father's, and they were still very much alive and well. Still, Arthur had a point, and as creepy as breaking and entering into a mausoleum seemed, I didn't fight him on it again. This was the only way to find out for sure.

"I can't believe we're doing this," I muttered under my breath.

As Arthur proceeded around to the back of the crypt, I frowned at the graves around me. A few inches from my feet sat a bouquet of fresh flowers leaning up against the mausoleum. It was a small bouquet—a mix of roses, carnations, and baby's breath in various colors held together by a simple red ribbon. They couldn't have been there long, for they were nearly perfect and not wilting. My eyes darted across the cemetery. Which

member of my family had these flowers been left for?
And by whom?

But the coast was clear. I read the names on the
plaque again of the deceased Worthingtons who'd
called this their final resting place. I didn't recognize
any of the names as family members who'd recently
passed. Could they still have family besides my own
who felt the need to leave flowers? Or was I seriously in
the dark about what laid beyond these walls.

A heavy metal door creaked open and Arthur came
back around, brushing soot off his hands. "That was
easier than I thought."

I looked at him in horror at what he had just done.
There was no telling what would be inside, and I
shivered at the idea of walking through something so
private and mysterious as somebody's burial chamber.

"Arthur, look at these flowers. Don't you think it's
weird? I looked at the plaque, but I don't know of any
of the people listed who could have passed away
recently."

He nodded. "From what I know, there hasn't been
a death in your family for decades . . . not since your
great-grandparents. And, let's see, your grandfather isn't
in any shape to visit, and your grandmother doesn't
exactly seem like the flower-leaving type. Even if she
was, I can guarantee you she would leave something a
lot nicer than these."

Around us, a breeze rustled the dead leaves on the
ground. I hugged my chest, suddenly strangely cold.

"I think I'm going to pass out," Abby said, her face
ghostly white.

"Sit down," I told her. "I'll go with Arthur."

"Keep an eye out for us," he said. "I'm going to
shut the door after we're in so no one can see."

She gave me a feeble nod and sat on one of the stone benches on the side of the mausoleum. Arthur peered around cautiously and, when he didn't see anybody else, led me around to the open doors.

My body stiffened, and I kept my eyes averted for as long as I could, petrified of what I would see.

He took the first step and then stopped until I followed. Despite my fear, the thought of finally getting closure pushed me onward. And before I could change my mind and turn around, Arthur pulled the doors almost fully closed.

I took a small step deeper inside the space and coughed; the air in the room was dusty and thick and had an unmistakable smell that could only be described as death. It was a claustrophobic's worst nightmare.

A large round glass window in the center of the ceiling allowed a faint beam of light to shine in the room, illuminating the dust. I let out a little whimper. Inside the space were several long rectangular openings stacked in the wall. Inside each was a coffin—most were clearly older than others.

I shivered as I watched Arthur drop to his knees and brush dust off a part of the bottom shelf. Then he shone his phone's flashlight over the area. I moaned and tapped my foot nervously.

"Magnus Worthington, empty as expected." He directed the light towards the shelf adjacent to my father's and my heart began to beat loudly in my ears. "Franklin Worthington. Eleanor. Hugh and Christabel Worthington. Warren and Louisa Worthington. Royce Worthington, Ruth Worthington, Olivia—all have coffins. Lillian Worthington . . . " He paused, then indicated a vacant opening below the above sarcophagus. "Empty."

"Oh!" I cried as I peered inside the rough stone vault. Instinctively, my hands flew up and covered my eyes, which had filled with tears of relief. My chest tightened, and I hyperventilated, the dense air making it nearly impossible to breathe.

Arthur's arms wrapped around me, hugging me as I trembled. Before I knew it, I was back outside, the cruel sunlight stinging my eyes. I keeled over and took several heaving breaths.

"What happened?" Abby leapt from her seat and an extra pair of arms embraced me.

"Her mother's spot is empty," Arthur whispered.

When I finally opened my eyes, my vision was blurry. I stared blankly ahead until the tears eventually ceased, my emotions completely numb as I struggled to process what I'd just learned.

But before I could fully comprehend that my mother might still be alive, that my family hadn't lied, a figure in the distance caught my attention. I squinted, wanting to be sure at what I saw.

Then I charged forward. "Hey!" I shouted, rage filling me from within. "You!"

But the old man made no attempt to run away.

Within seconds, I was in front of the man who I suspected was a lot more conniving than his unassuming appearance let on. "Why do you keep following me?" My eyes shot daggers at him. "What do you want with my family?"

"Was she there?" he asked, his eyes wide. "Did you find her?"

"What?" I gasped.

"Lillian—did you find her?"

The rage from my rush over dissipated as I stared incredulously at the elderly man who now had tears streaming down his cheeks.

"How do you—Who are—" Forming a sensible sentence seemed impossible. Then I realized that I had not answered his question. "It was empty . . . "

The look on his face was inexplicable, and I knew that so long as I lived, I would never, ever see an expression like that again.

"Who are you?" I asked more clearly this time, never expecting to hear the words that came next.

"I'm your grandfather, Meredith," he said. "Lillian is my daughter."

IN THE MOMENTS that followed, I felt as though the ground under my feet had begun to tremble, as though there was an earthquake rattling everything around me. The old man took a step forward and instinctively I stepped back.

"I've been searching for her for so, so long," he said.

When I didn't reply—the shock at what I'd heard rendered me speechless—he went on. "I never believed Lillian ran away. She would never have left you, Meredith. I know my daughter." His eyes welled with tears once more as he stared toward the mausoleum. "I never spoke to her after the day of that party. She had been so happy that morning—something about the tone in her voice gave me hope that she was finally breaking out of that depression she'd been in the last few months. She said she couldn't wait to show you off to the party goers, how happy she was for your father. I don't know what it was that changed, but I am certain of one thing: that was not the tone of someone who was planning to run away."

"Haven't you spoken to my father?" I managed.

"Your father has done everything possible to keep me out of his life, out of your life. I had my suspicions about him, and part of me still does, I'll admit. I made every attempt to contact him after he said that Lillian ran away, but all I got as an explanation was a copy of the letter she wrote. I wanted to know what happened, to find my daughter, but he went so far as to take legal action not to see me. He wouldn't allow me into your life, and I've spent years wondering where your mother was, if she was even—" He stopped, his breath catching before he continued. "Alive."

My knees threatened to buckle, so I bent to the ground and used one hand to steady myself while everything around me spun in circles.

"When I learned of your father's campaign, I had an idea. It was far-fetched to say the least, but I thought if I could just get to you, if Jack could just—"

My world stopped once more. "Wait—what?"

I looked up just in time to see him take a deep breath. "Please, Meredith, don't blame Jack. He only did what I told him—"

Before he could say another word, I was on my feet. "How do you know Jack?" I demanded, a fire of anger sparking inside of me. "Tell me the truth."

The man before me shoved his hands into his pockets. "Jack's family lives down the street from me in Canada. His father mentioned how he wanted his son to go to a good school in the States but that they couldn't afford it. I didn't think of it at the time, but eventually I struck a deal with him: I would pay for Jack to attend Harvard if he could work his way into your family for me and get my questions answered. I knew there was no other way for me to get in contact with you or your father. All Jack and his family wanted to get out of this was a good education, they had no intention or wish to harm your family. And all I wanted was information. It seemed like the perfect trade. Please, Meredith, understand where I'm coming from."

Slowly but surely, the story clicked.

"So Jack has been working for you all along?" My voice was steady and accusing.

"Yes," he replied quietly.

Not another word came out of my mouth before I spun on my heels and stormed away, burning tears spilling down my cheeks.

## CHAPTER 14

"Meredith won't get out of bed," I heard Abby whisper into the phone. She was in the bathroom adjacent to my room and I could only guess that she was speaking to Arthur.

"But I've tried everything!" she exclaimed, much louder this time.

And try everything she had. The only exception—the one I absolutely forbade her from doing—was calling Jack to give him a piece of her mind.

"Alright, fine!" I heard her say before she huffed and the door to the bathroom opened.

At first she appeared flustered until a forced smile appeared on her face. "Meredith . . . how would you like to go watch a movie at Arthur's? He's streaming a comedy that he's sure will take your mind off of things. You've been home for the last three days, surely a change of scenery will do you some good."

I turned to look out the window, my eyes focusing on a single pillowy white cloud that slowly crept along.

"Meredith—?" Abby said after a few long moments had gone by. "Can you at least blink so I know you're still alive?"

Hearing her cue made my lids close, the dryness of my eyes mildly burning. I turned to look at her. "I appreciate your constant supervision and Arthur's invitation but I'm really not in the mood."

Abby inhaled deeply. "Honey, I know you're hurt. What Jack did was the lowest level a human being could stoop to. But surely you've got to realize that maybe this is a blessing in disguise. Imagine if you had let things get even farther with him . . . I know that you were starting to feel something for him, but at least now you know the truth about his motives."

My eyes burned again but this time for a different reason. Tears pooled in my eyes but I was determined not to let them escape. "He could have called the whole deal off with my grandfather. If he really was starting to feel something like I was, he could have come clean—"

"Maybe he was scared of the consequences," Abby started, coming to take a seat beside me on the bed. "Look, by no means am I on Jack's side but this grandfather of yours doesn't seem like someone you'd want as an enemy."

I sat up a little straighter, wiping away the tears before they fell. Like they had so many times since I'd found out the truth, my emotions vacillated between the lows of sadness and the highs of rage. "I've replayed nearly every encounter with Jack in my head trying to find any indication that I missed his ulterior motive. I just can't believe he had the nerve to lie so blatantly to my face. It all makes sense now . . . the sightings of my grandfather when I was out with Jack— why, just the other day he suddenly appeared at Greyhurst after being discharged from the hospital and told me he had taken a *taxi*. I can't believe I was so stupid to miss the signs."

To Jack's credit, his every move seemed so genuine and sincere; I could have gone a lifetime without suspecting him.

"Don't blame yourself, Meredith. We all missed the signs."

I stared her directly in the eyes. "It is my fault for letting them take advantage of me. But I'm done being the pawn in their game. They can both go to hell."

STRONG WIND WHIPPED my hair as I stood on the dock, my jeans rolled up to my knees. My cloth canvas shoes lay abandoned on the edge of the tiled veranda where I'd kicked them off before stomping barefoot through the damp lawn. I imagined what they looked like sitting on the tile, lonesome and strewn about—those pristine white shoes, too clean to be exposed to the harsh elements of the outdoors, that were now exposed, *abandoned*.

They say ripping a Band-Aid off quickly is the best way to avoid pain. But what if the action of ripping it off causes a gaping hole so big that there is no Band-Aid big enough to cover it?

Over the last few days, I had recited my need to do this to myself over and over in my head. Unable to stop, I must have cried for hours each night before finally falling asleep on a pillowcase soaked with tears. Now, as I gazed out at the vigorous waves, I wished they could somehow sooth the fire that burned inside of me.

The rage I'd expressed to Abby was still coursing through my veins. My whole life, I'd encountered people who only saw me as a means to their goal. There was my father, who used me whenever a hint of doubt was cast at his involvement as a parent. My grandmother, who saw me as nothing more than a protégé who carried the last name she clung to so greatly. My supposed maternal grandfather, who had watched me from a distance for weeks and only came forward to find out what I'd seen in the mausoleum. And there was Jack, who saw me as a means to his stellar college education.

Despondent, I stared at the endless ocean before me, not moving at all except for the rhythmic rise and fall of my chest. I felt each slow breath and heard every wave, my mood quickly turning from livid anger to self-pity. Until the faint sound of footsteps caused my heart to skip a beat.

*Snap out of it, Meredith. You can't act like the victim.*

Eventually, the footsteps halted. It had to be Jack; I'd given him no room to decline my demand that he come. I took a deep breath.

"Were you ever planning on telling me about your generous scholarship to Harvard, or was keeping it a secret part of the deal?" My voice came across cold and unfeeling.

Gradually, I turned around, deciding that I actually wanted to see the look on his face. But seeing him ignited a physical force between us and I used all the restraint I had in me not to run up and envelope him in a dramatic embrace. Stupid feelings. Despite the hurt that I felt, despite the anger that was balled up inside, in front of me was a person I deeply cared for.

Our eyes met, mine seething, his large and unblinking. I watched as the frozen look of surprise wore off and his face hardened, his strong jaw now clenched.

"I don't believe it, is that why you have been avoiding me?" he remarked angrily. "He told you, didn't he? I can't believe he—"

"Can't believe he *what*? Can't believe he told his granddaughter that she was stupid enough to believe you?" I hissed. A lump formed in my throat, but I forced it down; crying was not an option now.

He threw his hands up in the air. "You didn't even know he was your grandfather until what, a couple days ago? I'm sure he conveniently left out the part about how he's been out to get your father since the day he announced his campaign. That little mishap that night of the gala . . . hate to break it to you, but your grandfather was the mastermind behind that."

The words hit me like a hard slap in the face, and I glowered at him. "He was only doing it because he thought my father had something to do with my mother's—with her running away."

"And for all we know he could have!" he shot back. "Don't you think it's a little strange that she disappears and not even her own father hears from her? Don't you think your father's aired recording sounded like the perfect confession? If you looked closely, I think you'd realize exactly what happened to her."

Tears welled up in my eyes. "My father loved her!" I cried. "I've watched him mourn her absence for years. The idea that he had something to do with her running away is sick and completely untrue. For all I know, my so-called grandfather who's been stalking me these last couple weeks could be some delusional old man who knows exactly where she is but is trying to sabotage my father's reputation."

Jack's expression seemed to soften. He took a step towards me, but I instinctively backed away. "Look,

Meredith, hear me out here. It's true; I took the job to do his dirty work. And it's true that he offered to pay for Harvard if I did it. But I swear to you, everything I've told you, everything I've shared with you, has been true." His eyes glared deep into my soul. "I never intended to hurt you. I care for you. Please believe me."

"You're a liar and a traitor, just like he is and just like my mother was," I spewed. "And I never, ever want to see any of you again."

A tear slipped free and rolled down my cheek. I quickly looked away, glad to break eye contact. If I stayed here much longer, I would lose control and cave into the emotions that threatened to consume me. Through blurred vision, I looked toward Greyhurst at the tall opaque glass windows and golden strings of light that looked so grand from where I stood, so perfectly regal, and knew my time here with him was over.

"Meredith—"

I held my hand up. "I don't want to hear it. I trusted you—" I turned to walk away, pausing when we were next to each other, our shoulders perfectly in line.

He spoke slowly, his voice cracking with each intricate word. "Well, it's clear your mind is made up." He took a deep breath. "Just know this, Meredith: I refuse to give up—I would never give up on you. Just tell me what I have to do to get you to trust me again."

Keeping my gaze focused ahead, I said the words that I wished I would never have to say to him. "Goodbye, Jack."

Then, without waiting for a response, I spun on my heels and ran towards the house.

"Meredith, don't—" His voice trailed behind me as I ran away, completely and utterly devastated.

FOR THE NEXT two weeks, I didn't take a single step onto Greyhurst's back lawn. To my grandmother's surprise, I allowed her to dictate my every move without protest; there was virtually nothing else to cling to these last weeks of summer and her overbearing ways suddenly seemed a welcome distraction from the betrayal I felt. Sensing that something must have been amiss but too proud to pass up an opportunity to achieve her mission, our grandmother went out of her way to ensure that no etiquette blunders would occur at the upcoming Fourth of July event as she instructed Abby and I on all the things a lady should not do.

A lady should not run or be seen walking hastily. A lady should never raise her voice or appear flustered. A lady should never begin eating before the head of household has started. A lady should not bare cleavage and should always make sure she has a weighted hem on windy days. A lady should never cross her ankle over her knee; legs should be crossed at the ankles only. The list went on and on.

All of that training could not have prepared me for the one thing that I dreaded more than the crowd of immodest guests I knew would be invited—having to venture outside Greyhurst's protective walls to where the party was being held outdoors.

Eventually, the day came, and after spending most of the day getting gussied up, I decided to venture outside before the event to survey the setup. As long as I knew all the detours I could take to avoid Jack—if he was still even working for my grandmother—I figured the night couldn't end too terribly.

Leaving Abby to finish getting her hair done, I carefully descended the staircase in my party heels and a floor length red ball gown and slipped out one of the side doors onto the smaller terrace. Although the event wasn't scheduled to start for another hour, festive music was already faintly audible from where I stood.

A warm breeze rustled up scents from my grandmother's rose bushes. I took a few steps forward to peer around the side of Greyhurst's exterior to get a better view of the outdoor arrangement, careful not to expose myself should Jack be in the backyard.

A large white tent had been erected in the backyard. From where I stood I could only see the side that was blocked off for the staff and realized I would have to go to the other side of the house if I wanted to see the guest entrance.

"Meredith—" came a voice from behind me.

I jumped. I would know that voice anywhere.

The instant I turned around our eyes met. "Jack," I whispered longingly.

He was handsomely dressed in a black suit, a red rose in his hand, and I almost allowed myself to acknowledge how good he looked in it, traitor that he was. His dark hair was longer than the buzz cut he'd sported all summer, this time it was combed to the side and slicked down. But despite his formal attire, his eyes appeared painfully sad, regret emanating from his features. His strong jaw was clenched at the sight of me, his brown eyes glistening, his lips drawn together. Gone were any traces of his dimples, of the way his entire face lit up when he smiled.

"You look beautiful," he remarked, his eyes moving up the length of my dress before settling on my eyes once more.

"Thank you," I said flatly. Hearing him compliment me so affectionately felt like a firing squad had just pulled the trigger on my heart.

A look of pain momentarily flashed on his face. "I've been trying to call you—"

"My phone's been turned off," I interjected.

His body stiffened. "Meredith, I know I screwed up. Believe me, not an hour goes by that I don't think about how much I hurt you."

He took a step towards me and I almost backed away.

I blinked back tears. "I'm leaving in two weeks and then you won't have to think twice about what you did." I tried to sound stoic, but my voice quivered.

His features softened, his eyes searching my face. "Meredith, I'm not asking you to forgive me right away, but I don't want this to be the end of us. You have every right to be angry—" He reached out to wipe a tear from my cheek. "Just don't give up on us."

"If you cared about me even a little bit you would have called off your promise to my grandfather, you would have confided in me. But you didn't," I whispered, turning my face away from his to avoid eye contact.

Suddenly, the door to the veranda opened and out came Abby.

"I've been looking everywhere for you!" she said, throwing her hands into the air. She too was dressed in a red gown, hers form fitting, a classic mermaid shape. She looked from me to Jack and back to me, her eyes widening.

"I was just about to leave," I said, taking several steps back from Jack.

"Meredith, please—"

But Abby stepped between us. "You heard her, she's done here," she said defensively.

"Abby, it's okay," I started.

"No," she interrupted, her hand going up. "I don't want him to hurt you more than he already has." She turned to Jack. "She trusted you, we all did. Meredith is like a sister to me and I will not let you or anyone else take advantage of her."

Tears flooded my eyes, ruining the expertly painted mascara and eye shadow that the makeup artist had spent over an hour applying, as Abby took my hand and pulled me towards the door. I took one last look at Jack's forlorn expression before the door closed behind us.

## CHAPTER 15

A short while later, after allowing the wave of tears to run their course and letting Abby work her magic to redo my makeup, I sat at one of the silk-topped outdoor tables under the long white valance that had been erected over the patio, affording a prime view of the expansive lawn. The party guests had begun to arrive, elegantly sauntering in and picking up a flute of champagne, appearing not to have a care in the world. How I wished I could also enjoy the festivities.

As I looked around the room at the hundred or so people, most of whom I had never seen in my life, my stomach twisted. The more I thought about Jack's betrayal, the more I pitied my father. Maybe he had tried looking for his own answers just like my maternal grandfather but nobody listened. Even now, as he embarked on the most important effort of his career, was there really anyone he could wholeheartedly trust? The constant schmoozing with people—was it really just dining with wolves who were waiting for him to become the main course?

"Something to eat, Miss?" asked the white-gloved server. He held an hors d'oeuvres tray in his hand with the option of escargot or Belgian endive with duck and apricot salad.

"No, thank you," I replied with a small smile.

"Champagne?" he offered, producing a bottle from the cart at his side.

"I'll have some iced tea, please," I said, spotting the pitcher on the cart.

The subtle clink of silverware could be heard as all around guests noshed on appetizers and engaged in small talk. All the while, I could merely stare down at my stack of untouched plates neatly arranged by size. The plates were white porcelain with a thick metallic gold trim that looked like they had been dipped in liquid gold, which, given where we were, very well might have been the case.

The sound of a clinking wine glass came over the microphone, and I looked up to see that it was my father.

"Ladies and gentlemen, allow me to make a toast." He raised his glass. "To prosperity and freedom!"

"To prosperity and freedom!" the crowd echoed, then the dance floor lit up, and the band played more upbeat tunes.

From behind the dramatic red and white floral centerpiece that sat on the table, I could see Arthur walking in our direction. He was in a white suit, a drink of some sort in his hand.

"Well, girls, don't you look . . . red," he said as he casually sauntered over to our side of the table.

I glared at him, unamused.

"Sheesh," Arthur said to Abby, gesturing at me.

"Leave her alone," she shot back. "You know what she's been through."

I felt an intense surge of gratitude toward Abby. She'd been nothing but protective of me all evening, going so far as to firmly, but politely, tell our grandmother that no, there was nothing I could do to get rid of the "hideous bags" that were under my eyes. Now she sat next to me, one hand lovingly resting on my arm.

"You, I knew, had been kidnapped and turned into a piranha ages ago. I just didn't know they'd gotten Meredith now, too." Arthur nonchalantly turned his head left and right, stretching his neck. "Regardless, I wanted to see if you'd do me the honor of having this dance, Abigail Nicole Preston. You look ravishing tonight."

Abby's mouth fell open. "I—"

"Go," I urged her. Whether she cared to see it or not, Arthur clearly had feelings for her. And if I knew Abby as well as I thought I did, I'd have guessed that somewhere deep down, she felt something for him, too.

"I'm not leaving you," she insisted.

"I'm fine," I replied. "I'm actually a little hungry, so I think I'll find something to eat." I didn't feel like eating, but I owed it to my body to put something in my stomach.

That seemed to do it—Abby had been after me to eat all day—because she sat up straight. "One dance," she said firmly. "And that's only because I pity you."

"Abigail," Arthur extended a hand and Abby gracefully rose out of her seat. Before he led her away, he discreetly slipped something out from his coat pocket and set it on the table by my side.

I waited until they were settled on the dance floor and couldn't see me before retrieving the manila envelope and carefully making my way through the crowd and back indoors. I had a hunch as to what was inside, and I wanted to be somewhere private when I finally unveiled its contents.

The house was quiet as I strode down the long hall that led to the foyer. When I reached the stairway, I held up the train of my dress and quietly climbed the stairs. The halls of the manor were dark on the second floor, the only light coming from the bright moon peering through the stained glass that lined the top of the windows.

When I reached my bedroom, I fumbled around for the light switch and then sat at my desk. I took a deep breath, then undid the metal clasp and pulled out the program Arthur had found at Herkimer.

The moment I touched the paper, a bolt of energy surged through my fingertips. My mother had held this very paper in her hands and now, well over a decade later, I was doing the exact same thing. The contents of the paper were nothing special. In fact, the agenda looked a lot like tonight's party or any other Worthington party for that matter. I turned it over, not expecting to see anything but wanting to soak in every inch of the document. On the back of the program were four very familiar numbers. My heart skipped a beat. Without thinking twice, I pulled the desk drawer open and picked up the stack of photos I'd taken from Herkimer. When I found the one I was looking for, I held it up next to the program and gasped. The same four numbers—9298—were written in exactly the same handwriting as those on the back of the picture.

Had my mother written these numbers? That would have meant that she too had seen these pictures. My father's words echoed in my mind. *She could spend hours lost in the shelves.* My mother had been an art history major, and she loved the library. Had she tried to investigate Herkimer's past? Had her curiosity led her to the very place where I'd found these photos? Rita from the antique shop had suggested that the numbers might have been part of a library archive of some sort, and now I was beginning to think she was right.

I stood up and began to pace. Although I was trying to keep myself from thinking of Jack, something he had said was bugging me as well. *If you looked closely, I think you'd realize exactly what happened to her.* What if he was right and the answers I was looking for were right under my nose. There had to be something in this house, some trace of my mother somewhere. I knew so little of her, and with my parents living here for as long as they did, I figured there had to be some remnant of her. Could Greyhurst's library hold the answer to these mysterious numbers?

With my family safely distracted outside, I made my way out of my room and back down the dimly lit hall. It felt like forever before the seemingly infinite number of doors gave way to the large entrance that led to the library.

As I entered and flipped the light switch on, brightness filled the space. In the far corner was an older Steinway piano, not as large as the one in the great hall, but elegant just the same. Two armchairs sat on either side of a round table with a stained glass lamp in the far right corner by the bookshelves. In the center of the room was the library's focal point, the deep cherry wood desk that my father sat at in the mornings. The real history, however, lay in the massive dark wood showcase, which lined an entire wall. But I wasn't here to marvel at the antiques. Instead, I scoured the bookshelves, searching the spines for numbers that matched the four on the photo.

Finally, I found one that matched.

*American Genealogy.*

"Interesting choice," I whispered as I pulled it out and rifled through the pages. Before I could catch it, something small fell to the ground with a clamor.

I looked around the floor, and sure enough, lying mere inches from my feet was a small brass key.

"How on earth am I going to figure out what this belongs to?" I asked out loud.

I bent over to pick it up and sighed in frustration, then slumped into one of the armchairs beside the tall plant in the corner of the room.

After everything I'd unearthed so far, I still felt as if I was nowhere near figuring out how the pieces fit together. In all reality, I didn't even know what problem I was chasing. Was it the fact that Herkimer was not what people thought it was? That Jack had been attacked there, or that he was working with my mother's father this whole time? That all this time, while my mother was thought to have run away, her father had been searching for her? And to add to everything there was the mystery of why her belongings would have been found hundreds of feet across the ocean on that island on the very night she was never heard from again.

As I stared blankly ahead, my eyes fixated on the patterned wallpaper. For several long moments, I didn't move a muscle. The burning urge inside of me that ached to know what happened to my mother was subsiding as disappointment set in. Just as I was about to force myself to stand, I saw it: hardly visible between the diamond-patterned wall panels was the faintest looking break in the pattern—a keyhole. I lifted my finger to touch the spot, running it over the slight raise.

My attempts to pry the panel open were unsuccessful; the lock clearly required a conventional key. My adrenaline soared—could it be?

Barely able to see the keyhole, I blindly moved the key along the wall until I felt it slip into the lock. *Please, please let this work.* Then I twisted it, but nothing happened. No, *no*! I banged my hand on the wall, wincing from the pain I hadn't intended to cause. Groaning, I pushed at the panel, willing it to open, and watched with wide eyes as part of the wall shifted, revealing an entryway.

The space before me was dark, but in the distance I could see a faint glow of light. Slowly, I inched forward, until the ground beneath my feet suddenly dropped.

I'd reached a staircase.

I descended the invisible flight of steps one by one. When I finally reached the bottom, I coughed. The air was thick and musty, but thankfully the light was getting brighter. I used the walls as a guide, the texture crumbling beneath my touch. Oddly, I heard water slosh across the floor as I walked, and I wondered where this passageway could possibly lead.

Eventually, I reached a glowing pyre that stuck out from the wall and with a small tug, it dislodged, providing me with a portable light. I carried it as I continued to walk, the hallway seemingly endless. Tempted as I was to turn back, I kept on. Surely the pathway led somewhere or else what was its purpose?

What started off as a hesitant walk turned into a jog and then an all out run as my inner fears began their cruel whispers. Even if I'd wanted to turn back, by now I was probably closer to the end than I was the beginning. What if I got stuck? Abby had no idea where I was, nor did Arthur or my grandparents. For all I knew, I could be trapped here for all of eternity with no one to hear my cries.

But an unexplainable force drove me forward.

I stopped to rub my sore shoulders, letting my dress, which was now damp, fall to the floor. I leaned against the wall, needing a moment to regroup. There had to be a light at the end of this tunnel—wasn't that what I was supposed to tell myself? I hadn't the faintest idea how much longer I would have to walk to reach the end. There was a big possibility that I was on a bridge to nowhere. This wasn't what I had in mind—what had started off as looking for evidence of my mother's time at Greyhurst had unintentionally sent me on this wild excursion.

I stood up straight and forced my tired legs to continue on. Eventually the hallway curved to the right, and I had a feeling I was getting close. About fifty steps later, I was relieved to see a rickety set of stairs before me. My heart skipped a beat as I held the pyre closer. I said a silent prayer, ascended the steps, and pushed the double doors above me open, shining the light into the darkness that was behind it.

"Hello?" I called, just in case I wasn't alone.

When no one answered, I took several hesitant steps forward. The light lit up enough of the area that I could see the side of a house. I frowned, trying to figure out why I had the sudden feeling of déjà vu. Then I let out a gasp, the light nearly falling from my hand.

I was standing outside the Herkimer mansion.

A MILLION THOUGHTS raced through my head. An underwater tunnel leading from Greyhurst to

Herkimer? How was that possible? And more importantly, *why*?

As I looked up at the house, I could see a faint glow of light coming out of one of the upstairs windows. If my memory of the layout served me correctly, I could swear it was the library. A chilling thought came to mind: that light—could it be the same light I saw from my bedroom window? It had to be. Which meant . . . was somebody inside at this very moment?

Thinking of what happened to Jack was almost enough to send me back the way I'd come. *Jack*. Saying his name in my mind felt like a bullet to the heart. Part of me needed convincing that I wasn't here to fight his battle. I was close to uncovering something that could potentially unveil what became of my mother; this had nothing to do with Jack. I'd simply come too far to back down now.

Leaving the doors to the tunnel wide open, I proceeded quietly through the grass to get a better view of the window above. My backup plan was simple: if needed, I could charge back the way I'd come and would be back at Greyhurst in no time. In theory, it sounded effective; in reality, I knew I was going out on a limb.

Step by step, I inched toward the front of the house until my foot kicked something through the grass and an expletive escaped my lips. The bell landed a few inches away between two others that were in the grass. Shining the pyre in front of me, I bent over to examine the bells. These couldn't be from cattle—it just didn't seem plausible. All throughout Herkimer I'd seen traces of bell decorations in the intricate carvings, antique bells in the curator's cabinet in the upstairs antique room, multiple bells beside the place settings on the downstairs table.

I reached down to pick one up as I thought about it, careful not to move the clapper enough to produce another sound. Then I stopped. Beside the bell was what looked like a piece of jewelry. I tried to pick it up, but it was lodged in the earth. Tugging, I felt it come free and I stumbled back. Rubbing the dirt off with my fingers, I watched as bits of grass and leaves tumbled back to the ground. As I held the light up to it, I couldn't help but feel a strange, familiar sense of déjà vu; in my hands was a sapphire bracelet, the unique twisted pattern was uncanny. I knew I had seen it before, but where? I stared off toward the blackness as I forced myself to think. Looking at it again, it slowly came to me.

It was a piece of jewelry that my mother was wearing in the picture Arthur showed me from the party. I had studied that photo for hours, pouring over every detail of the mother I never knew.

My stomach did somersaults. She really must have been here. I hadn't doubted Arthur finding her program here, but a big part of me thought it could have been a mistake. There were a million possibilities: maybe it had been swept away in the water and washed up at Herkimer, maybe someone planted it here on purpose as a ruse. But now this piece of jewelry changed everything. Maybe this is why I'd felt so drawn to Herkimer all summer . . . maybe I sensed something, or—

Suddenly, gravel crunched behind me. My breath caught in my chest, and my entire body froze. Before I could muster the courage to turn around, everything went black.

# CHAPTER 16

What felt like an eternity of deep sleep later, my mind awakened with a whooshing roar in my ears. Where *was* I? My eyes were closed, the throbbing pain radiating from my head making it impossible to think straight. At first I thought I was swimming, only to realize I did not feel wet. It took several long moments for my thoughts to sort out and return me to my last conscious memory. There was my encounter with Jack, the party, the tunnel to Herkimer—the whoosh in my ears turned into a high pitched ringing as my eyes fluttered open, and the next few memories came rushing in. A cry escaped my lips. I had been attacked!

Complete blackness surrounded me. Panicked, I tried to pull myself upright, but then gasped when I found that I couldn't move an inch. Earth crumbled between my fingers as I felt the area around me. I screamed. I was completely enclosed between four walls. No, I was buried. Alive.

I kicked and thumped, but I couldn't roll over, I couldn't do anything but feel the four walls that surrounded me, encased me, wouldn't let me leave.

Terror coursed through my every cell, claustrophobia making my heart flutter with panic.

"Help!" I screamed. "Help!"

But nobody would hear me. Nobody even knew I was at Herkimer or how I'd gotten here.

I was going to die. I knew it more than ever. The more I screamed and panicked and cried, the more exhausted I became.

Through my cries, I heard a faint noise above ground. When I stopped moving about, the sound stopped, too. I moved my hand, the only part of my body that had room to move, and sure enough, the sound was back. It sounded like something rattling.

It was a bell.

In my panic, I hadn't noticed that something was tugging at my index finger. Running my other hand over it, I felt a ring of thick string tied around my finger, which I traced upwards.

It didn't take long for the realization to hit me like a speeding train. Of course! Why hadn't I thought of it sooner?

Years ago, in middle school, I had found a book of creepy stories at the library that my friends and I read a passage from. The page I read was the story of a cemetery watchman who'd heard screams in the nights following the burial of a young woman. It said that people who died in the Victorian era used to request bells be tied to their finger in case they were buried alive. The Victorians were preoccupied with death and were mortified at the prospect of being buried alive. Designated individuals, like this watchman, would alternate shifts camping out by the gravesite waiting. But this woman had not had a bell and, terrified that it was a spirit haunting him, the man never came to her aid. Days later, when the sounds stopped, he ordered the undertaker to exhume the grave, and what he found was terrifying: the woman had indeed been buried alive, but it was worse than that. In the grave was a baby with evidence to show that the woman thought to have been deceased had painstakingly delivered while underground.

Thinking of the story again produced a new wave of terror. If only I had someone watching out for me. Whoever had done this to me knew that no one would hear. I tugged at the string around my finger. It was my only hope. I had to hold out hope that somebody— anybody—would know what this sick person had done to me.

My oxygen supply would run out before I knew it. Tears ran down the sides of my face and onto my ears as I continued to tug. Who else had met the same fate? With all the bells scattered across the lawn, it was mortifying to think of how many others there were. My mother had to be one of them, of that I was sure. She had to be. She wouldn't have disappeared like that. But how was I going to prove that if I didn't make it out alive?

Before I realized what was happening, a delirious lightheadedness began to set in as oxygen depletion took effect. Within moments, I began to fall into a deep, hazy sleep.

I WAS SWIMMING. No, I was flying. Or maybe floating? I felt light and free as though I was soaring through a brightly lit space. Was this heaven?

All of a sudden, the gliding sensation I felt subsided, and I was hanging, suspended in the brightness for what felt like eternity. My stomach dropped as I suddenly fell through the nothingness. The bright white light faded into different shades of gray. Light gray turned into dark gray, which turned into infant shades of black.

Would I never reach the bottom? The descent was rapidly accelerating, and now I felt faster than light. My body plummeted further and further until I hit the bottom, and complete blackness overcame me.

"MEREDITH! MEREDITH, WAKE up!"

I felt myself being shaken.

*Leave me alone*, I thought, my eyes rolling back into my head as I battled the urge to drift back to sleep. But then—wait.

I was alive.

My eyes fluttered open, and through the blur I saw a shape huddled over me.

"Thank God!" the man cried out, and I felt myself being pulled into an embrace.

The voice sounded so familiar.

"What—?" I murmured, but stopped because my throat burned.

I raised a weak hand to my neck and rubbed the skin, which was excruciating to the touch. Around me everything was dark. Where *was* I? In the distance, an eruption of sound and color spread across the night sky. Slivers of starlight glided along, their life spanning only seconds until they dissolved into tragic nonexistence.

Fireworks, the party, the tunnel. As memories trickled back, my heart began to race in panic.

"We have to get off this island," the person said, and I felt my body rise, shaky hands under my back and legs.

When my vision cleared, I saw my maternal grandfather before me.

"Put me down!" I demanded, then forced my way out of his arms and ran back to the spot where I'd been hit, sinking to the ground and desperately combing my hands through the grass. "I can't leave. My mother is here, I know it."

Sure enough, lying in the grass was the sapphire bracelet I'd found earlier. "Oh, mother," I cried. "Who did this to us? I'm so sorry I never put the pieces together—that no one saved you."

Several feet away, I saw the hole in which I had been buried.

Uncontrollable sobs wracked my body. I shivered from an intense feeling of cold that I knew only I felt. My life felt like a thousand-piece puzzle, one that I worked so hard to complete despite the fact that the biggest piece—my mother—was missing, and now it was a convoluted pile of parts once more. Everything that I'd known to be true about my life was now jumbled, broken. My eyes filled to the brim with tears, and I cried so hard it was practically a wail.

My grandfather hugged me to him, and despite all the hurt I felt, I didn't have the strength to move away. "Meredith, we have to get off this island. Once we're safe, I promise we will find out what happened to Lillian. I promise . . . I've spent years trying to find out, and together we will get closure. But right now I won't risk your safety."

Deep down in my core, I knew he was right, but to leave felt as though it would physically break my heart. "I just—I don't want to leave her—"

I sunk down onto the ground just as another deep cry from within left my lips.

Once more, I felt myself being picked up from the ground, but I didn't protest; I was too emotionally broken to react.

"She never would have left you, Meredith," he said as he carried me toward the boat.

I only half heard his words on the way back to Greyhurst. My mind wandered in and out of conscious thoughts, and before I knew it, I was standing on the dock, my grandfather beside me, leading me back toward the party.

"I can't go back there," I said to him, my knees buckling as I slumped to the ground. The upbeat music and inebriated laughter was too much to bear. Much like a vehicle being forced to pull the emergency brake, my physical emotions were shutting down one by one.

"Meredith!" a girl's voice called in the background. But I was only half aware; I was slipping fast, practically unable to keep my head upright.

Before I knew it, I felt myself being cradled seconds before I was to hit the ground.

"Meredith, Meredith!" Abby screamed. "What happened to her?"

Tears flowed from my eyes as I heard my grandfather recount what had happened to me. Hearing it from someone else made the reality unbearable, and it was as though the life had been sucked out of me.

"No," Abby sobbed as she hugged me to her. "No—"

I wasn't sure how long we sat crying on the grass, I only knew that it felt like an eternity before I forced myself up and dragged my achy limbs toward Greyhurst.

We were approaching the house when Arthur rushed toward us. "Thank God you're alright, Meredith. Have you seen Jack?"

My first instinct was to react to hearing Jack's name, to allow myself to feel concerned.

"He probably didn't tell you, but I told him off before the party. I haven't seen him since," Abby confessed to Arthur.

But Arthur's head shook in fierce disagreement. "No, he was here a little bit ago. I spoke to him, and he asked where Meredith was." He turned towards me. "We looked for you but you were nowhere to be found, and I realized you might have gone back to Herkimer after I gave you that envelope. Jack said he was going to look for you there—he was worried—and for us to keep a lookout here, but that was well over an hour ago."

Jack was worried about me? He had tried to find me? I replayed the night's events in my head. I didn't see him at Herkimer. Maybe he was inside the house or maybe he hadn't yet arrived? Or—

My eyes widened in shock. No. No. No.

"Oh my God," I whispered, then I turned to Arthur. "I have to go back to Herkimer!"

THE MOUND OF fresh dirt nearly made my heart stop as I raced across the lawn at Herkimer. A search of the front lawn where I had been attacked showed no sign of Jack's grave. But my core told me to keep looking, and sure enough, around the back of the house was that unmistakable heap.

"Jack!" I screamed as I manically scooped the earth away. "Jack!"

"Stand back," Arthur commanded, finally joining me with a shovel in hand. Abby had stayed back at his suggestion to fend off any questions as to our whereabouts and to keep a lookout should Jack somehow show up. But now, seeing the fresh dirt before me, I knew Jack would do no such thing.

My body shook as I watched Arthur peel away at the grave. When he was certain he was close, he dropped to his knees and furiously scooped the remaining dirt away.

Shining the light into the space, I saw Jack lying with his eyes closed, his body deathly still. A whimper escaped my lips as Arthur threw himself onto Jack and lifted him upright.

For several long moments, I stared, paralyzed, waiting for a single movement of his hand, a flutter of his eyelid—anything—that would indicate that he was still alive. When nothing came, I pushed Arthur aside and breathed into Jack's mouth, forcing as much oxygen as I could get into his lungs.

But his body did not respond.

## CHAPTER 17

"Arthur, he's—" But I couldn't say the word. My knees buckled, and I slumped to the floor, my body shaking so hard my teeth chattered.

"Meredith, I—" But even he couldn't speak as we both stared at Jack's lifeless body.

"I should never have accused him. Now he'll never know how I truly felt, how sorry I am." The words were spilling out of my mouth, and although they were directed at Arthur, it was almost as though I was willing Jack to hear them. "He can't be gone."

Arthur swallowed, and his eyes looked dark. "He cared for you or else he never would have come here. You can't blame yourself."

But I did. "It's all my fault, Arthur. If I had never come here, if I had never involved Jack in this mess this never would have happened." Imagining the possibilities was so bitterly painful, like a flickering moment of hope that was crushed with the reality that was right before my eyes.

My sobs turned into wails and then desperate gasps for air. In those long moments, I experienced a full range of grief: sorrow, shock, disbelief, and anger. But the fury over his death was the most profound.

"He can't be gone," I said resolutely as I began administering mouth-to-mouth resuscitation once more. My heart kicked fast and hard in my chest.

"Mere—" Arthur's arm was on my shoulder, gently pulling me away. I could hear his voice crack as he said, "I'm afraid he's . . . I'm afraid we are too late."

"No," I said, jerking out of his grasp and pinning myself to Jack.

After several more mouthfuls and forceful pumps to his chest, a quiet wheeze made my adrenaline soar. Could it be or was I imagining things?

I continued breathing into him, until finally, Jack gasped. His eyes fluttered open as he struggled to fill his chest with fresh air.

The rush I felt at the sound of his breath was unexplainable.

"I can't believe it!" I cried, so relieved that I began to weep.

"Meredith," Jack whispered, his voice raspy. But it was the sweetest sound I'd ever heard.

"Are you okay? Are you hurt?" I scanned his body for any traces of injury. Arthur was at my side, his jaw open in shock as he lifted Jack's head. "I'm so sorry, Jack, I'm so sorry for everything."

It took him several moments to fully open his eyes. When enough oxygen had refilled his lungs, he pulled himself up and reached to stroke my hair. "I saw Bill attack you, but before I could—"

My ears began to ring.

Arthur took a single step closer. "Wait—what did you say?"

Jack nodded his head. "It was Bill, Meredith's driver. I'm a thousand percent sure."

"That makes no sense," I whispered. Surely a member of the staff wouldn't betray us like this. "Why would Bill—?"

"I have no idea, but I really think we should . . . " He paused and took a deep breath of air. "I think we should get out of here."

"I agree," Arthur said. "Let's go before something else happens and there's no one to find any of us."

He looked toward the boat, and that's when I remembered something.

"We don't need the boat. I found an underwater tunnel that leads from Greyhurst to Herkimer. When I went to the library earlier I found it by mistake and that's how I ended up here." I watched as they realized what I was saying.

"It's too dangerous," Arthur said finally. "Bill could be lurking in that tunnel."

"He's not," Jack said. "He came on a boat; I saw it leave Greyhurst and thought it was Meredith, so I followed it, but out stepped Bill."

"See," I started. "Then the tunnel is definitely a better way to get back. Come on, let's go!"

FINDING THE DOUBLE doors that opened to the stairwell proved challenging. The fake patch of grass matched the lawn so perfectly that it literally took scanning the ground inch by inch to notice the faint discrepancy.

The tunnel back towards Greyhurst was dark as we blindly made our way down the corridor until we reached the final stretch. I shuffled to a halt and Jack skidded into my side as muffled voices echoed from the library on the other side of the wall.

Jack grabbed my hand as we tried to make out the conversation through the thick wooden doors. "And the legacy lives on once more," the voice said. What followed was the most cryptic laugh I'd ever heard. It was a deep, throaty laugh with not the slightest hint of remorse, like someone who could—and would—kill again.

"The little wench was no different than her mother. And that gardener, who did he think he was outsmarting?" The man laughed again. "How fitting are their lonely resting places . . . so close but yet so far from one another. Let them spend all of eternity knowing just who they've wronged."

Fire ripped through me, and just before I could charge forward, Arthur's arm reached out to hold me back. I looked at him desperately and pushed him away, but he held tight. He shook his head firmly, telling me what I knew he would say if he could speak aloud, "NO."

Then he swung the stick he'd picked up over his shoulder and took a quiet step forward. Nothing but the curve in the tunnel separated us from this terrible murderer.

Were my father and grandparents in danger? My stomach dropped as I realized how fooled we'd all been.

I slowly edged forward, craning my head to see into the door of the library. From my vantage point, I could see Bill. The traitor. Who else was he talking to? It was clear that he was working with somebody, but I didn't recognize the voice. From where I stood, it was impossible to see. I leaned back and mouthed Bill's name to Jack.

"What do we do?" I whispered. "Do we corner them?"

Jack looked pensive. "You stay back, I'll go in first." He leaned forward as if to listen closer, but Bill and his accomplice said nothing. Instead, I heard the quiet shuffle of feet. And then an unmistakable whimper.

Jack advanced to get a better view of the room. With wide eyes, he gestured for me to join him.

I let out a muffled scream. In the corner of the room stood Bill. Beside him was Abby, slumped on the floor unconscious, her arms tied, blood caking on her face.

AT THE SOUND of my scream, Bill's head jerked around, and he charged toward us.

I flew back and Jack's arm pulled me as we ran down the hall through the darkness, my knees weakening with every step. The footsteps behind us grew louder, and I knew Bill was gaining speed.

*I need to call my father*, I thought frantically as I forced myself to gain momentum.

We rounded the corner so fast that I nearly slid into the wall, but quickly swerved and continued forward.

"HELP!" I shouted. "HELP US!"

"Keep running!" Arthur shouted from behind. Then I heard a sickening crack, and he went quiet.

Jack and I continued to run, but it wasn't fast enough. Suddenly, something clasped around my ankle, and I was flying. I hit the hard floor with a painful thud that knocked the air from my chest. Two strong hands grabbed me tightly by the arms and pinned me against the wall.

"Don't touch her!" Jack barked protectively.

"One more word, and she dies right here," my attacker hissed, and I saw the glimmer of a gun in his hand.

"I swear you'll be sorry. You won't get away with this!" Jack spewed.

Bill let out a menacing laugh. "Somehow I don't believe you." He waved the gun back and forth between us. "Both of you, in front of me, arms up in the air. Now!"

I waited for Jack to join me, and then we both walked in front of Bill, who kept the gun pushed into my back. When we reached Arthur's slumped body, I winced as Bill struck him again with a crushing blow to the head.

Tears welled in my eyes.

*Please be okay, Arthur.*

When we reached the library, I braced myself at what I would see inside. But nothing could have prepared me for the sight of Bill's accomplice. Wearing a polished suit and looking more alive than I'd ever known him to look was my paternal grandfather.

# CHAPTER 18

"Grandfather?" I cried out. "What—I don't—Why—" I was completely and utterly dumbfounded. What was my grandfather doing here? Did he really know what Bill had done to us?

Grandfather opened his mouth, and what came out was the most perfect sounding, crisp set of words as though he had never suffered a stroke, as though the health problem plaguing him for well over a decade had never existed.

"You don't know what you've gotten yourself into, Meredith, and I'm afraid this has to be the consequence," he said.

The fact that he could speak shocked me like a bullet to the chest.

Before I could respond, Bill threw me into a heap on the floor next to Abby. I slumped forward, my hands clutching the floor as I gasped for air.

"The consequence for *what*? You tried to kill her!" Jack lunged at him but was held in place by Bill. When he struggled to break free from Bill's grip, he too was fiercely knocked back against the wall. I winced as his head smashed against the sheet of glass from the picture behind him. It shattered with a loud crack, and he let out a painful moan.

Bill bound Jack's hands tightly with a rope and stepped forward to do the same to me. After he finished, he brushed off his hands and took a step toward my grandfather.

"Every family has secrets," my grandfather said. "This one is no different."

Shock coursed through my body, but Jack . . . I could see the rage emanating from him.

"You son of a bitch! How could you sit back and have your own granddaughter killed?" He glared at him, his eyes piercing.

Jack's outburst was the final straw. Bill lunged toward him, and I watched in horror as he struck Jack over the head with a candelabra, rendering him unconscious. Tears sprung to my eyes as I struggled to comprehend what was going on. Around me, my best friend and the person I'd fallen in love with were unconscious on the ground. And my grandfather had tried to kill me.

My grandfather gestured to Bill who proceeded to the closed library door and turned the key in the lock. I gulped, my pulse racing in my throat as I came to a horrifying conclusion: that key had just sealed my fate.

He rose from his spot. "If you must know, I can tell you. But don't think it doesn't come at a price. Bill might not have succeeded the first time, but I can tell you that I have been very efficient in the past."

A choked sob escaped my throat. "How could you do this to us? You destroyed my father's life! What kind of a father are you?"

His eyes seemed to shoot daggers at me. "*I* destroyed his life? You have no idea what his life would have been like if our secret had gotten out. He would have been reduced to nothing thanks to that nosy mother of yours. He'd have no career, no campaign, no money, nothing!"

He took a menacing step forward.

"The Worthington family name has been powerful for centuries, Meredith. What would people think if they found out about us, if they found out that . . . " His lips twisted and he frowned. "That none of us who write that name to paper are true Worthingtons."

If he had been expecting a response to that statement, he didn't get one from me. True Worthingtons? That meant nothing to me. Fury pounded in my ears. "It's not for you to make that decision," I spat back. "You cannot kill thinking that other people care about this name, about this family's legacy. No one would want to be associated with a legacy that you've tarnished so badly."

He let out an evil chuckle. "You say that. Your mother thought she was onto me. Much like yourself, she was quite adventurous. She thought she'd discovered something digging through Herkimer like she did; she found the passage here at Greyhurst, and for that I applaud her—when I had it commissioned I made sure it wasn't easy to find. Although it did cost her the ultimate price. How she cried when I made her write that final letter to your father."

He looked like he was reminiscing, and I wanted nothing but to scream. He was reminiscing about my mother's final moments, about moments that I had wondered about for years.

"How many people have you done this to?" I cried, boiling hate erupting in my chest.

"In my lifetime? You will be my second. Your precious friends will definitely up my number. Surely you all found Herkimer very entertaining this summer . . . I take it you read the diary that you found? Or rather, started to read."

My mind closed; I couldn't remember a single word that I had read, be it from the diary or any other book. "What does that have to do with anything?"

"Well, since you're nice and comfortable, let me tell you a story. In the 1800s, the Worthington family lived at the Herkimer mansion, or Bellevue as it was called. Just like we are today, they were one of the most powerful families of their time. The house was just one of the many owned by the Worthingtons then. My grandmother worked as a servant for the family."

He walked over to one of the library shelves and pushed a book, a small panel springing open. Then he reached inside and pulled out the familiar looking diary that I had first seen at Herkimer.

"This journal chronicles her experience, but it doesn't even begin to cover the half of it. She was beaten, tortured, her skin worked raw every single day. All of this was in front of her son—my father—who had to witness the way his mother was subjected to such cruelty, the way she was tortured and cursed at. Every time they rang that pitiful little bell to call her to her next beating, he knew he had to make it stop. One day, he gave the Worthingtons what they truly deserved. And it didn't take much to trick them into thinking poor little Henry died of consumption. It didn't take long for him to exterminate the entire family. He'd learned enough about them over the years to know exactly where their true assets lie. A couple of forged documents later, and he was one of them. He became as much of a Worthington as the dead corpses that still lay buried around the property. How they must have felt . . . buried alive with nothing but the tolling bells to hear."

The inside of my mouth felt as though it was packed with cotton balls. A huge swell of disgust and nausea rose inside me. Bellevue . . . so that's why I never found anything about Herkimer online! And the reference to Henry's death—was he the child in the post mortem picture I had found? The diary entry I read mentioned he had been sick. I was lightheaded at the words, but he didn't stop.

"My father entrusted this to me on his deathbed, and nobody, not even you, will change that. It is my duty and a duty of every member of this family to protect our secret. And I, just like my family before me, have vowed to uphold my promise. I've kept the media at bay about Herkimer's history; turns out starting that fire was just what I needed to convince them it was haunted. I kept my word to my father when I discovered what your mother knew, and I will do it again with you."

I was tempted to cry, but felt too numb. My mind struggled to process his words; I had so many questions, but had no idea where to begin. "Does my father know?"

"When I feel that the time is right, he'll know. Or perhaps I'll die before then and he'll have nothing but the note I've written to guide him."

I felt a small tinge of relief. Although I was descended from a bloodline of killers, at least my father was not part of it all. Yet.

Jack and Abby still lay slumped by my side, and as my eyes concentrated on them, I was relieved to see that they were still breathing. But Arthur . . . Our fate was now in my hands. I needed to set my emotions aside; right now, my primary focus was on getting us out alive.

"Why do you care so much?" I asked, realizing that to make it out alive meant I needed to go into survival mode. "Why do you care so much about the Worthington name, about the money?" I asked again. "Why not be noble, be the one who comes clean? You could be a hero."

"If the King of England abdicated his throne, he would still be royalty. If I relinquish this family name, I would be nothing. I would have nothing."

"You have the chance to change now; you don't have to kill anyone else," I pleaded.

"Don't listen to her," Bill said.

Fire rose in my chest, and I shot him a dirty look, disgusted at myself for ever thinking highly of him. But how could I have known?

"Oh, but of course I do, Meredith. Bill, the jewelry," my grandfather said.

"Yes, sir," Bill replied, and I thought he was headed my way but instead he bent over Abby and violently stripped all of her jewelry from around her neck, ears, and wrist. It was then that I realized that my own jewelry was no longer on my person. "Quite a collection you're accumulating," Bill marveled.

My grandfather laughed. "Quite a different style from the pieces already amassed." He turned to me. "Although you won't live long enough to make this a valid lesson, my father made it a point never to leave any artifacts of his victim's identity behind. Clothes fade and disintegrate, but jewelry is much too permanent. Bill here will have some gardening to do tomorrow."

Bill set Abby's jewelry on the desk beside a heap of jewels that I recognized as the set I wore earlier. Just when I thought this web couldn't get any more tangled, I realized that the box Abby and I had been researching all summer was nothing more than a collection of victims' jewelry. RC. I didn't want to tell him that the box was now in my possession, so I'd have to phrase my next question carefully.

"So if we aren't Worthingtons by blood, then what is our family name? What was your father's name?"

"Royce Cook. Otherwise known as son of the Worthington family slave."

Out of the corner of my eye, I saw Arthur peer out from the tunnel opening, and my heart skipped a beat.

"That had to have been hard," I fibbed, trying to keep their focus off of Arthur. "I can see why he would do what he did."

My supposedly paralyzed grandfather walked to the window. His intense gaze made it clear he was reminiscing, but I cared little for his sentimental moments. Instead, when I was sure Bill's back was towards us, I looked at Arthur and gestured toward the door.

He nodded, and I wondered if he was ever unconscious at all. I threw a fleeting look at him, and ever so quietly, scrambled to my hands and knees as our captors looked away. Inching across the marble floor to Jack's side, I began to pick at his ropes, my hands concealed behind my back.

The sound of Arthur scurrying across the marble caused the two men to look up in surprise. Then, before our enemies realized what was going on, Arthur dashed toward the door.

"NO!" Bill yelled, and before Arthur had a chance to turn the key, a gunshot pierced the air. Arthur let out a blood-curdling cry and clutched his stomach as he collapsed to the ground.

Bill charged toward me, rage emanating from his eyes. Whatever anger he had pent up inside had just exploded after Arthur's attempted escape. His hand swept across the bookcase shelves as he stomped across the room. Books flew off in every direction, glass artifacts shattering across the floor. When he was mere inches away, he pulled me up by my shirt and let out a blood-curdling howl.

"How dare you think you can outsmart me!" Bill shouted as he gripped me by the neck.

"Don't!" I wheezed.

From the corner of my eye I could see Arthur's movements slowing, blood soaking through his shirt. His breaths appeared sharp and painful.

Rage and panic tore through me and before I could think twice, I tipped my head back and then came forward, biting into Bill's flesh as hard as I could, my teeth penetrating the layers of his skin.

He screamed and kicked me away, writhing in pain. I stumbled back, my neck throbbing. I clutched my face in my hand and looked up at the two men before me, contempt radiating from my eyes as I took deep, labored breaths to lessen the excruciating pain.

A second later, Bill was back, and I watched in horror as he struck an unconscious Jack with a crushing blow to the chest.

Jack collapsed backwards in a silent heap, a trickle of blood oozing down his forehead.

"Let's see you help him, too," Bill spewed.

Tears ran down my cheek as my grandfather advanced toward me. "So you think you can save your friends from their plight, do you?" His voice was penetrating and methodical, hatred laced in his even dialect. When I said nothing, rage filled his voice as he hissed. "Do you!"

I shrunk into the wall.

"No," I whispered feebly.

A twisted smile formed at his lips, all traces of wrath now erased. "That's better. We wouldn't want you to be disobedient, would we?" He took a step back, his hands clasped together as he surveyed the room.

"You know, I had planned to kill you all together. But I realized that watching your friends squirm just a little bit longer would be even more satisfying." He paused. "It would seem that Arthur wants to make this even more enthralling. And I'm not opposed to such tantalizing games, although they do get messy."

"Don't you dare," I warned, unable to contain my rage.

"Oh, not to worry dear girl, you'll all be resting peacefully by morning. Do send your mother my regards." His expression seemed to relax as fire boiled inside me. He was a lunatic, a warped human being. No amount of devotion to his father would have driven him to do this. No, this was the working of a true psychopath.

"I hope you rot in hell," I said, unable to disguise my contempt.

He made slow, deliberate strides until he was mere inches away from me. "What an ungrateful little brat you are. On second thought, why not give you your happy mother-daughter reunion just a little bit early, shall we? After all, I still have the gardener and your friends to finish off."

"No," I whimpered.

"I'll count down if you prefer, give you time to think your final thoughts." Then he raised his hands into the air and encircled my neck. I caught a brief glimpse of his entire face up close, and although my mind was much too consumed with the million thoughts racing through it, for a split second I realized how unrecognizable he looked.

"One." The grip of his hands tightened ever so slightly.

My eyes widened in horror as I came to the abrupt realization that I was going to die.

*Oh, God! Somebody help me. Please*, I silently pleaded, *I don't want to die.*

"Two." Tighter.

My mind went blank, and an eerie sense of submission at my impending fate washed over me.

"Three." His hands squeezed forcefully now, and I savored every last molecule of precious air.

"I love you, Jack," I tried to say.

But no words came as the light faded into blackness.

# CHAPTER 19

A body bag was the first thing I saw when my eyes fluttered opened. Behind me, I heard whispers and faint footsteps, but I could not so much as move my gaze a millimeter away from the lifeless corpse that lay mere feet from my legs. Memories of where I was slowly returned, and I realized with increased panic just who might be lying before me.

The medical cot beneath me creaked as I pressed into it to push myself up. I pulled the oxygen mask off and with a dizzying twist, looked around the room. Abby. Arthur. Jack. None of them were anywhere to be seen. A puddle of blood marked the floor where Arthur had fallen, another pooled by the desk. My heart lurched when I saw the two individuals standing in the doorway of the library, looking as solemn as I'd ever seen them.

On the right was my father, his eyes bloodshot as he talked to a uniformed paramedic, and I would never forget the look of relief that came over his face upon seeing me awake.

"Thank God," he exhaled. The next thing I knew he was by my side, and I was wrapped in his tight embrace.

"Meredith!" my grandmother said. Her face muscles were tense, her eyes wide. She took several hurried steps toward me.

"Where is everyone?" I demanded, pulling away from my father. "Who——?"

My father opened his mouth to speak, but my grandmother put a hand on his shoulder to stop him, and then said, "It's your grandfather. Everyone else is fine."

I couldn't find words to express my relief. Tears streamed my face as the paramedic checked my vitals, eventually announcing that I was all right. My father and the paramedic each reached an arm out to help me stand. Pain radiated through my limbs as I shifted forward onto my legs. "Come, dear, sit down," my father said.

Wobbling, I took several steps until I reached one of the two armchairs and collapsed into the closest one. The tension in the room was so thick that it was almost dizzying.

"You won't believe what he's done——" I started, mystified as to how I could possibly even begin to tell my family what I'd discovered and sure that I'd be called a flat out liar.

My grandmother reached out to stroke my cheek. "I know."

The shock of her words struck me like a crippling blow. My eyes bore into hers. The horror of my grandfather's involvement in my mother's death had completely blinded me to another possible truth: that my grandmother was just as involved.

As though sensing that my rage was beginning to take flight, she said, "Believe me when I say, dear child, that I never, ever knew of what Edwin did to your mother."

"Your grandmother saved you and your friends," my father said.

Shocked, I looked back at her. "You . . . you saved us?"

Her eyes misted over. "I heard his entire confession outside of the door. At first I didn't even realize he was speaking. But it didn't take long for me to recognize his voice, it always was so distinct." Her voice trembled, and I watched as my father put a comforting hand on her shoulder.

"When I realized what was happening, I ran to retrieve my gun. You all were unconscious when I finally made it back. I saw hands around your neck, and I couldn't think straight. I just knew I had to save you and I . . . I shot him in the leg." Tears trickled down her cheek, and I almost thought she was done with her story, but then she said, "Your grandfather reached for his own gun, and I ducked for cover thinking he was coming for me but he . . . he—oh God I can't—"

For several long moments, she buried her face in her hands and sobbed. Then she looked up at me. "He pulled the trigger. On himself."

My eyes widened as I looked from my father to my grandmother in shock. Despite the fact that he was a cold-blooded murderer, my grandmother had just watched her husband die before her eyes. "Oh, grandmother—"

"Not a single word, young lady. I cannot for a second believe the monster that he was—" The sight of tears flowing from her eyes was one I never imagined I would ever see in my lifetime.

"Where is Bill?" I asked, suddenly fearful that he had gotten away.

"The police just left with him in their custody," my father said. "Your grandmother shot him in the shoulder."

"He charged towards me after Edwin pulled the trigger," she explained.

For the first time in what felt like an eternity, I let out a sigh of relief. "And Jack, Abby, and Arthur are all right?"

"They are fine, shaken up of course, but fine. Arthur is being treated for a gunshot wound to the abdomen but he'll be all right. The police are talking to Abby and Jack as we speak," my father said, wrapping his arms around me. "Whenever you're up to it, they will want to get your statement as well, but there's no rush."

My heart ached for Arthur. I took a deep breath. "I'm ready, but I honestly don't know what I'm going to say. My thoughts are so scattered and nothing makes sense . . . "

My father squeezed me tighter. "I'm still trying to put the pieces together myself."

Before I could reply, Jack and Abby burst through the doors. "Meredith . . . " Jack said as he came toward me, and I went from my father's arms to his. Abby joined in on the hug, and together we stood in a solid embrace, no one needing to say a word.

THE NEXT DAY, before my uncles were set to arrive, I reconvened with my grandmother and father in the tearoom and at my request, my grandmother told us the story of how the biggest decision of her life ultimately turned out to be so terribly regrettable.

"The man I met in my twenties is not the same person you knew in recent years. He was charming, charismatic. I was never after his family name or the money; all the girls in town would have agreed that Edwin had such a good soul that he could have been a poor man." She paused, her eyes staring out the window, and I watched as her mouth formed a small smile at the memory.

"We lived happily for many years as we raised the children and he worked to further his career. His father passed away the winter after Magnus turned five; his mother had died when he was a teenager. It was apparent that his father's loss affected him profoundly. He would often talk of making his father proud, of working to honor his memory. To me, he simply seemed ambitious, and I admired that. In hindsight, I suppose it was more an obsession than a goal. Being a Worthington was everything to Edwin. As time went on, I felt him become more and more distant, but assumed we had reached the point in our lives when that was normal. Our children were grown and out of the house, and we each had our own interests. I gave him space and busied myself so his absence didn't feel so apparent."

She turned to look at me.

"Your mother's disappearance was one of our biggest disagreements. I didn't understand why she would leave and was hurt, but Edwin appeared angry, and he made it no secret. I was not to speak of her in his presence, and he championed me to help your father realize he had been betrayed. She had been going through a rough time emotionally—I still blame myself for not making her feel more at home. Greyhurst can be a desolate prison if you don't armor yourself against its lonely walls. I had every intention of reaching out to her after she left, to see if I could help, even if it meant she never returned to your father. But Edwin demanded that I leave things be; he showed me the letter she'd written and insisted he would not let her demean the family's name with her actions. It was like her existence was virtually shut out of our lives at his command. After his stroke nearly a year later, I felt too sorry for him to go against his word, but I have spent years wondering what became of her . . . "

"He said his father made him promise on his deathbed that he would protect their new identity," I said. "Why did they have to go to such extremes for something so meaningless?"

"My dear, if I've learned one thing over the years, it's that money is a drug that makes people do terrible things. I am guilty of my own share of dishonorable actions, nothing so drastic, but shameful just the same. At a certain point it makes you feel superior, like without it you would be so very ordinary, and it seeps its way into your every move and action, every decision becoming a way to further your power. Money was also the way he was able to manipulate this story of Herkimer. He was the one who fed me the story of Herkimer's past; I can only assume that he fooled the media into thinking it had never been lived in."

"So father would have been the next in line to carry out his wishes . . . "

My father reached for my hand. "Perhaps that's why he never spoke of it. I would never have accepted, and he must have known it." He gazed out the window, his eyes welling. "How I wish my dear Lillian didn't have to fall victim to his actions. I am so very sorry, Meredith."

I threw myself into his arms in an embrace and tried to hide the fact that tears were pouring down my cheeks. "No, I'm the one who is sorry."

THERE WAS NOT a cloud in the sky the day of the funeral. It was a sunny July day, an uncharacteristic seventy-five degrees. Looking outside, you would never know that the days leading up to the burial had been any different. But an uncanny storm with black skies and unrelenting rain had plagued this small coastal town for the last four days. The calm ocean waters I now saw from my window had before been roaring with life, crashing against the dock in a strong fury. Inside Greyhurst, a similar atmosphere was present. And while the family had bonded together in many ways, the unspoken truth was that we all seemed to be processing our emotions using vastly different means.

But now the day was finally upon us. Tucking my clutch under my arm, I took a deep breath and proceeded downstairs without giving second thought to the emotions I'd tried to keep at bay. In choosing what to wear, I decided against black; too much death had occurred as a result of my family that it only felt right to break tradition. Instead, I wore a cream colored suit, a way to show my decision to celebrate life.

A caravan of cars left Greyhurst and headed to the church where our family gathered to pay their respects. The masses that had wanted to attend had been politely turned down. At my father's request, today there would be no cameras, no interviews or media of any sort—we would be a new kind of normal for the day, a family remembering. Just before our car came to a stop, I felt my father and grandmother each reach for one of my hands and in the moments before the doors opened, we sat in silence, our grasps tight.

We quietly assembled inside the church where the priest said a few words of support and a prayer. In a rare change of events, my family gave no speeches; no one vied to stand on the podium for a typical Worthington show. Candles were lit and heads bent in prayer; my surroundings felt so surreal that I couldn't help but feel like my own movements were out of body. I was only vaguely aware of my family that filled the pews behind me.

My uncles and their wives, Abby and her family, and people who I had not seen in years but who were in some way related to us all came together. Before long, it was time for the burial and as we walked across the lawn my strides felt long, my every footstep pronounced. Around me family proceeded out of the church silently, heads bowed, through the grass and the tombstones to the tent that had been placed over the spot where the shiny wooden casket adorned with a large mound of flowers lie.

I tried my best not to look at the flowers for fear of seeing the word I had printed on the sash. It was a word I barely knew how to use, one that resided only in my imagination: mother. In preparing for today's memorial, I learned so much about the woman I'd so longed to know. The outpour of support from the community was extraordinary, a tribute to someone who had been so cherished and respected. Even now as we gathered in a circle together, a breeze blew and I was almost certain that she must have been looking down on us. I prayed that we were doing her memory justice.

Her final resting place was simple: a modest plot for two that she would someday share with my father. The family mausoleum that had become the eternal home to so many Worthingtons was now sealed off following my grandfather's interment. Keeping with my family's decision to honor the dead, this would not be the last funeral I attended. The lives of those who died at my great-grandfather's expense would be honored individually and given a proper burial.

As we waited for the spiritual words of the funeral prayer to commence, I looked to my father and saw him locked in an embrace with my mother's father who I had only begun to get to know. Since the horrific discoveries at the last gala, he had become an integral part of our healing process. My father and grandmother welcomed him with open arms and much needed amends were made. He was invited to stay at Greyhurst with us indefinitely, and in a strange way it felt like he had always been a part of my life. Still, to really know someone took time, but now we had all the time in the world.

The priest began the prayer, and in the final moments before her coffin was lowered, a ball formed in my throat.

"Goodbye, mother," I whispered.

I reached out to touch the casket, knowing that for the rest of my life this would be as close as I would ever get to my mother.

Before retreating, I reached into my suit pocket and pulled out a letter that I'd written her, tucking it into the floral arrangement.

Once the service was over and we all said our proper goodbyes, I knew my time in Hyannis Port had come to an end, and it was time to head home. With one final glance back at my mother's grave, I let out a contented sigh. After so many years, she was finally given the resting place she deserved.

## CHAPTER 20

*Take a deep breath*, I told myself as I walked up the white marble steps of the oversized grey building flanked on either side with massive rows of Corinthian columns. Behind me, thunder rumbled in the already overcast sky, sending me scurrying up the stairs.

The last few months had flown by. My father won the primaries, giving him a pretty good outlook on today's election, and naturally my whole family was very pleased.

Life for the rest of us slowly returned to normal, or as normal as possible after the onslaught of the summer. The seemingly immaculate life that we lived would go on as it had for generations, and it was ironic, unsettling even, to think that my grandfather ultimately got what he wanted: an intact Worthington family. In an attempt to right the wrong of so many decades past, my father made every attempt to find the rightful owners of our estate but learned a sad truth: the real Worthington bloodline had been cut short by my great-grandfather's heinous acts. Over a handful of people had died to give us the name we had today—of which no heirs survived—and I knew we would all spend the rest of our lives trying to find a way to make sure their memories were validated.

It was hard not to carry that truth with me everywhere. Even as I walked down the hall of the boarding school I'd attended for years, I felt like a much different person. The road to redemption would be one walked slowly, but we would get there. We had to.

"Psst," my friend Morgan whispered from behind me just as I pulled open the door to room 501C, Mr. Poligala's morning chemistry class.

"Hey!" I said, desperately wanting to climb under a rock.

"The big day is finally here! I'm rooting for your dad," she said.

"Thank you. I appreciate your support," I replied, finding a seat and taking out my books. Today's graded exam was going to be challenging, and I could use a few extra moments to review.

She raised an eyebrow and put a hand on my shoulder. "You look a little off. You okay?"

I gave her a reassuring smile. "It's just nerves. And this test really doesn't help."

Her expression softened. "I'm surprised you're even here today. I have no idea how you're going to sit through class. I would be dying. But at least it'll sorta be a distraction, right? Text me later and let me know how things are going."

"Absolutely," I said, burying my nose in my chemistry book.

MORGAN COULDN'T HAVE put it any better. The school day, which already felt like a chore to begin with, crawled at a snail's pace. I was pretty sure I bombed the quiz; no amount of studying could have countered my nerves. By the time the bell rang in my last class, I was already one foot out the door to the parking lot. The drive from Connecticut to our home in Wellesley, Massachusetts typically took around an hour, but today I had a little detour to make before I returned home and Abby arrived.

Outside, the rain had subsided, leaving much cooler weather in its place. To tune out my own relentless thinking, I turned on the radio halfway through my drive. "The temperature is now a chilly thirty-nine degrees as a cold front moves through eastern Massachusetts. Stay tuned for more information." Then the headline news began to air.

Great. A cold front. I was dressed for rain, not cold. Unconsciously, I pressed harder on the gas pedal, turning my seat warmer and heater on high.

When I pulled through Harvard's distinguished gates a short while later, a wave of excitement coursed through me. Jack's class would be ending shortly, and I couldn't wait to tell him my news. I drove down the tree flanked road to the ancient brick building that I recalled Jack saying was the undergraduate hall when he'd given me a tour a few weeks back. I parked in a visitor's spot and powered off the car. I stepped out and shivered—it felt much colder than thirty-nine degrees. Looking around, I saw people bundled in coats. My jeans and light raincoat weren't enough, but I simply shrugged, then quickly ran to the sidewalk where Jack was sitting on a bench.

"Hey," I said. "Have you been waiting for me long?"

"Just got out," he replied with a smile, then he kissed me passionately on the lips.

I kissed him back, but I couldn't stop shivering.

"Jeez, Meredith, cold much?"

I laughed through clenched teeth. "No, not really."

"Here, take my jacket," he said.

I put up my hand to stop him but he was already slipping out of it.

"No, Jack, you would freeze! I'm fine, really," I protested once more as he wrapped it around my shoulders.

But he didn't take the jacket back. Instead, he gently took my hand and led me to the neighboring building, a brown brick structure with a large outdoor stairway.

I frowned. I had a reason for coming here and it took all my restraint not to blow the surprise. "Where are we going?"

"I'm getting you a warmer jacket. And a winter hat. And gloves. I'm used to the cold . . . my flimsy jacket is going to keep you warm all of two seconds."

Once inside, we walked into the Harvard gift shop and Jack scanned the aisles. He gestured toward a maroon Harvard jacket. "There's basic Harvard, or we can go a little more specialized." He smiled as he pointed past the generic items to the racks with different department gear.

"You're jumping the gun. I was planning on surprising you a different way." Then I pulled a folded piece of paper out of my jacket and waved it excitedly. "Guess what this is."

I let him think about it for a few seconds before I held it out to him.

He unfolded the paper and read aloud. "We are pleased to inform you that your application to the undergraduate Biology program has been accepted."

Jack looked up at me, his eyes widening. Then he swept me off my feet and spun me around.

I laughed, a huge smile plastered on my face. "It's official, I'll be joining you at Harvard next fall! I found out last night . . . early admission."

The look on his face was priceless. "And biology— was your dad okay with it?"

My smile widened. "He was more than okay; he encouraged me to go for it. I still can't believe it . . . "

Jack enveloped me in a hug once more, the feeling of his arms around me making me melt. "I'm so proud of you, babe. You're going to make an amazing doctor."

Then he raised a mischievous eyebrow and smiled. "This makes shopping a whole lot easier." He pointed to the far right of the store and I spied the words "Harvard Medical School" on the rack. "This way . . . "

THE KNOTS IN my stomach twisted just a little bit tighter as I pulled into the large roundabout in front of our estate a short while later and powered off the engine. I sat in the car and looked out the window. Cars were parked outside the gates, and I knew there were many hungry photographers waiting to get my photo. I took a deep breath and looked away at the garden around the side of the manor, the fall flowers turning brown after the nightly frost.

As always, leaving Jack's side was agonizing. After his exam, he would be at my father's event, and it couldn't come fast enough. My family was due at the DCU Center in Worcester in a few hours to wait out the poll results, which meant that as soon as I went inside I would have to begin getting ready for what would surely be a televised event. My father had cast his vote when the polls opened this morning and had spent the rest of the day greeting voters and trying to make his final pitch. My grandmother and uncles, who had arrived a few days ago, spent the morning at the venue overseeing the last few details. Even Arthur had skipped class to assist. Now everyone was surely scrambling to get ready. The last of our caravan—Abby and her family—were expected to arrive in the next half hour.

With a deep breath, I made my way inside, where I proceeded to shower and slip on the grey pinstriped tailored dress made just for tonight's event. I went through the motions of getting ready, each task filling me with more trepidation. With all that my father had endured these last few months, I desperately wanted him to win. He'd poured his heart and soul into this campaign; I would be crushed if he was defeated.

After pulling my hair back into a low bun, I wandered back to my closet and pulled out a pair of simple black pumps and my heavy black coat. The intercom in my room sounded, and I pressed the receiving button.

"Your father is ready," our housekeeper said.

I made my way downstairs to find Abby and her family in our foyer, their bags being carried inside by the staff. After exchanging hugs, it was time to leave.

An hour later, our limousine pulled up to the massive convention center. Hundreds of spectators—and protestors—lined the streets. As the limo door opened, we took turns stepping out into the chilly November air.

Father graciously waved to his supporters while myself, my grandmother, uncles Charlie and Ephraim, Abby and Arthur stood on the sidelines. My grandpa

Martin had even come down from Canada to show his support.

Event coordinators ushered us inside to two large adjoining private dressing rooms that father's campaign team had already taken the liberty of setting up. Each of us were handed a patriotic American flag pin, which I fastened to the lapel of my dress. Then we planted ourselves down in front of a large flat screen TV and waited.

"The polls are now closed," the newswoman announced a little while later. Exactly one hour and fifty-two minutes after closing time, it was final.

The newscaster reappeared on screen. "The results are in. Leading by 79,425 votes, the winner of the Massachusetts gubernatorial race is . . . Magnus Worthington!"

Cheers rose up in the room as the television panned to a chart of the tallied results. Tears pricked my eyes as I hugged my father.

"Thank you," he whispered in my ear. "I could not have done this without your support."

I pulled him closer. "You had this in the bag from day one. I'm so proud to be your daughter."

After celebrating the good news, it was time to address the state. He was promptly given a final dab of powder and had one last pep talk with his advisors, and then a cue signaled that the audience was ready.

It felt like a blur as we gathered behind the access door leading to the giant arena and lined up in order of importance—how that was determined I wasn't really sure.

The doors opened and my father stepped into the arena to the sound of shrill screams and applause. I blinked, taking in the thousands of people that were in my peripheral view, each of them fervently waving a tiny American flag about.

I followed behind my uncle Charlie and took a seat in the coveted front row immediately behind the podium. A camera crew was centered in on my father and I prayed that I was not within shot. The shock of his win still had not sunk in and I knew when it did, there would be many more tears—of both relief and happiness—to shed.

My father stood at the podium while the audience continued to howl. As the noise began to die down, he clasped his hands together and spoke.

"Great people of Massachusetts!" His voice came over strong and powerful.

The crowd went wild again.

"Thank you for having me here today. I am both proud and honored to represent this great state as governor."

My family clapped, and I emulated their motions, overcome with stage fright. I'd never been on TV prior to my father's political career, and while I had never been front and center, I still never became accustomed to the idea of being on public display, even if only in the background. To keep calm, I gazed at Jack, who sat in the front row of the crowd beside my grandpa Martin. He winked at me and clapped, and I couldn't help but smile.

I directed my attention to my father's speech. "I first want to thank each and every one of you for your support during this most challenging and competitive campaign—"

Although I had been mostly certain he would win, now that it was final I found myself wondering what that would mean for our small family. I was grateful that my father had this victory, grateful at the chance for him to start fresh. I settled back in my seat and let out a content sigh. No matter what the future brought, no matter what this new role meant for our dynamic, at this moment everything was exactly as it should be.

LATER THAT NIGHT, after we had enjoyed a joyous celebratory dinner and dessert, the party was finally winding down.

Jack and I wandered outside after eating, and I was sitting on his lap admiring the quiet waves of the nearby waterfront when Arthur came flying outside in a tizzy.

My stomach did somersaults. What was he up to now? "Arthur, what's wrong?"

"Where's Abby?" he asked, his brow glistening.

I pointed to the bench adjacent to ours. "She was here a minute ago but ran inside for a second, why?"

"I just . . . I need to talk to her," he stammered.

"Need to talk to who?" Abby was standing behind Arthur.

He turned around. "You."

Her face flushed as she peered back at him. "So . . . talk."

"I can't put it off any longer. Abigail Preston, will you go out with me?" Arthur spat, his voice loud and nervous.

Jack and I let out quiet chuckles. Abby was laughing herself, her face bright red as she too tried to suppress it.

"Oh, Arthur," she said when she saw his shoulders slump in embarrassment. "I hate to say it out loud, but yes, I will."

That's all Arthur needed to hear to literally sweep Abby off her feet and seal those words with a kiss.

* * *

THE WIND ON the island whipped around us as we walked its border, our steps in perfect sync. A couple months ago, I swore I never wanted to see Herkimer again. My grandmother was now back to living at the family estate in Newport, Rhode Island and like the rest of my family, had no plans to return to Greyhurst. But time brings peace, and with the historic Herkimer mansion set to be demolished in a few days, I knew that part of gaining closure would be facing its sight one last time.

Jack held my hand tightly, not just to steady me from the ice that crunched beneath our steps, but for reassurance that I was holding up. All of Herkimer's victims were now exhumed. As we passed the uneven patches of grass where the bodies had once laid, I couldn't help but feel how different the atmosphere on the island was. My earlier visits had always felt like there was a calling, something yearning to be discovered so that justice could be brought. Now, it felt so *quiet*.

After much discussion on what should take the place of such an iconic building, my father decided that a serene garden would be the perfect tribute to those who'd lost their lives. Complete with a gazebo, benches, and lush walkways, the plans illustrated a serene haven, the complete antithesis of what had always been the island of Herkimer.

I reached my free hand into the pocket of my coat and toyed with the antique amethyst earrings that belonged to one of the victims. The box Jack had unearthed—and its valuable contents—had been turned over to the Massachusetts Historical Society. And while

I might someday decide to donate these earrings so that they may rejoin the other pieces, I was simply not ready to part with them yet.

Taking a deep breath and letting my lungs savor the air that filled them, I turned to Jack. "You know, I never asked you if you knew who called the Coast Guard that day you were attacked here."

"Martin told me it was him. He always had a premonition that something bad was going to happen. He was looking out for us, I guess."

"I can never repay him," I said quietly. A sentimental lump formed in my throat, and I knew that part of the reason was saying goodbye to this place that had come to have so many moments, both good and bad, that had forever changed my life.

"I guess we should get ready to head back," I said, swallowing down the lump in my throat. My whole family was invited to my grandmother's annual Thanksgiving get-together in Newport, including my grandpa Martin and, of course, Jack.

We stopped walking, and Jack turned me to face him. At first, he simply held me in his strong, muscular arms, looking into my eyes. "I know how hard this must be for you—not just today, but every day that you've wondered, every day that you searched for answers. The future will be different; it will be better. And I want you to know that I will be here for you through it all."

I stood on my toes to get closer to him, then I held his face in my gloved hands.

Jack smiled, and when we kissed I literally thought I was flying. When we finally parted, we started, arm in arm, for the dock.

Midway through our walk, Jack stopped. He then bent down and picked up something small from the grass that glimmered in the day's light. He frowned as he held it out for me to see.

I gazed down at it and felt dizzy. In his hand lay a tiny heart earring with the trademark diamond center that only I would recognize: it was the earring I realized I was missing that morning with Abby.

The dream I'd had the night before Abby's birthday, the old woman, the graveyard, my laryngitis— my head filled with visions that twisted together like a complex sailor's knot. My heart beat wildly inside my chest. It just didn't make sense. How did the earring end up here? I hadn't been anywhere near Herkimer the day I wore these.

I recalled the words the wrinkled old woman had said, "You will fall." Since then I had indeed fallen. I had fallen into a deep, dark hole. But just like the dream, I'd also gotten back on my feet.

"Interesting," I said simply.

When I showed no interest in taking it, he shrugged and tossed it back into the grass. "Oh well, just another Herkimer mystery."

But I knew it was no mystery. The earring, like the house, would be gone in a few days, and I realized that I was all right with that. I could have taken it back to the matching piece that sat in my jewelry box. But I decided against it. This earring would represent the part of me that would go down with Herkimer, because there was no denying that part of my soul was being demolished with its walls. It would represent the part of me that was forever attached to the house.

Jack's hand reached for mine once more and in that moment I knew.

Despite the part of me that would forever remain with Herkimer, I never felt more complete than I did today.

Visit Natalie on the web at
www.natalie-merheb.com

Made in the USA
Columbia, SC
14 January 2023